THE BIGGEST HEART IN CHOCTAW HOLLOW

THE BIGGEST HEART IN CHOCTAW HOLLOW

•

BERNADETTE PRUITT

AVALON BOOKS
THOMAS BOUREGY AND COMPANY, INC.
401 LAFAYETTE STREET
NEW YORK, NEW YORK 10003

© Copyright 1997 by Bernadette Pruitt
Library of Congress Catalog Card Number: 96-95280
ISBN 0-8034-9190-5
All rights reserved.
All the characters in this book are fictitious,
and any resemblance to actual persons,
living or dead, is purely coincidental.

PRINTED IN THE UNITED STATES OF AMERICA
ON ACID-FREE PAPER
BY HADDON CRAFTSMEN, SCRANTON, PENNSYLVANIA

THE BIGGEST HEART IN CHOCTAW HOLLOW

Chapter One

"Grandmama, you promised not to cry."

Brooke Adler took a fresh handkerchief from her grandmother's maid, Hannah, who knew from thirty years of experience that the old lady would turn on the spigot. Brooke touched the lace-trimmed Irish linen to the old lady's rouged cheeks.

Ingrid Crosswaite gave a little sniff, then struck a hurt pose, one that Brooke knew all too well. She'd used it to manipulate two generations of Adlers and Crosswaites. "May heaven forgive me for allowing my precious granddaughter to go off into the wilds all alone," she whined. "Hannah, dear, please get my blood pressure medicine. Hurry."

"Yes, Mrs. Crosswaite," the maid said quickly, giving Brooke a knowing look.

"With some Evian water, please—chilled," the old woman whimpered.

"Certainly," Hannah said. "I know just how you like it."

Brooke's stomach churned with a mixture of annoyance and guilt. "Please, Grandmama," she said, touching Mrs. Crosswaite's arm, "I'm going to southeastern Oklahoma, not Borneo."

The old lady gave the handkerchief a few nervous twists as she paced over the black and white marble tiles of the foyer. "There are animals of prey in those mountains. And possibly outlaws. And what if I have a heart attack from worrying about you?"

Before Brooke could respond, Hannah returned carrying a small red capsule in a tiny paper cup and the Evian in a Waterford wineglass.

"Oh, just in time," Mrs. Crosswaite said, collapsing dramatically onto a straight-backed chair with fussy, carved legs. She emptied the cup into her palm and with a hand as steady as a sharpshooter's, placed the pill on the tip of her tongue. She took a sip from the crystal goblet, then handed it back to the maid with a sudden and exaggerated tremor. "It's all right," she said, placing a hand over her breast. She took a few deep breaths. "My, what a close call. I could almost see my life passing before me—white light at the end of a tunnel."

Hannah, a plump woman in her sixties with short, curly gray hair, patted her on the shoulder. "Mrs. Crosswaite, you're going to be just fine." She turned to Brooke with a conspiratorial twinkle in her vivid blue eyes. Everyone in the household but Grandmama knew that the little red pills were placebos. The doctors—and there had been many of them—had all told

Brooke that the heart of Ingrid Crosswaite, age seventy-two, was as sound as a dollar.

"Grandmama," Brooke said gently, brushing a wisp of elegantly coifed silver hair from the old woman's temple, "let's go in the living room for a moment and sit. You'll be more comfortable."

Brooke took one of her grandmother's elbows and Hannah took the other, steering her past the two suitcases Brooke had set by the door. They guided her to her favorite armchair, a plump affair covered with blue and white striped twill, which the decorators had assured her would be perfect with the large old Persian rug. Hannah removed Mrs. Crosswaite's black patent pumps and put her feet up on the striped ottoman.

Brooke sat on the corner of the large footstool and gave her grandmother's ankle a gentle pat. "I know you love me and want only what you think is best, but we made an agreement. If I can prove within a year that I can be self-supporting, I'm free to give my trust fund to charity. I'm free to live a normal life like everyone else."

"Dear, I just don't understand," the older woman protested. "I've given you . . ."

"Grandmama," Brooke interrupted, "money has not bought this family happiness and you know it."

"You don't know what you're talking about, child. My mother was poor once and she said she'd never forget it."

Brooke shook her head stubbornly. "And I've only been rich. I want to be free of country clubs, tennis clubs, charity balls, the false suitors, and all the obligations and pretensions of high society. I want to make it on my own, Grandmama, to be an artist, to teach others to appreciate art, to earn my own paycheck. It's nothing against you. I love you. We're all each other has left. But you're of a different era. You can only be happy inside this gilded cage. I think I would be happier outside of it. And we agreed. If I can't make it on my own, I'll come back and take over your role managing the family affairs—both financial and social."

The old lady smiled weakly. "Yes, dear. It's because I love you that I'm giving you this chance. But to talk about it and to see you walk out that door are two different things. My heart can barely stand the strain."

"I'll miss you, Grandmama," Brooke said. "I wish I could be more of the granddaughter you always wanted—one who has embraced the society life as you have, as Mother did."

"Nonsense," Mrs. Crosswaite said. But Brooke detected a trace of disappointment in her voice. "Somebody has to be the family bohemian and it might as well be you."

Brooke got up and kissed her grandmother on the forehead. "It's time for me to go."

The old lady put her arms around her granddaughter and returned the kiss. "Will you forgive me if I don't walk you to the door?" she asked. "I don't want to tax my heart."

"Yes, Grandmama."

"You're leaving me in a delicate condition, you know," she said, patting her chest.

"Perhaps I should get Hannah to call Dr. Halpern.

Maybe you should cancel your plans to go to the symphony tea tomorrow," Brooke suggested.

"Oh, no," Mrs. Crosswaite quickly countered. "I'm sure a good night's rest will do me wonders. I could never shirk my duties."

Brooke struggled to conceal her amusement. "Of course not, Grandmama." She kissed the old lady once again. "Remember, I love you. I'll call as soon as I get settled. It may be a day or two. If there are any problems, you'll hear from me sooner."

She turned and quickly left the room before the lump in her throat turned to tears.

Hannah was waiting in the foyer. "Honey, I know you got what it takes," she said. "I knew it from the time you were eight years old and you threw off that party dress to help Ned paint the garage. As for your grandmother, she'll be fine. Just leave it to Ned and me."

No sooner was his name mentioned than the front door opened and Ned, Grandmama's butler, stepped inside.

"I couldn't let you run off without saying goodbye." A sad smile appeared across his thin, Scottish face. "Here, let me help you load those suitcases."

Brooke stood by as he placed them in the trunk of her little red Miata. The inside of the car was crammed with art supplies. Extra clothing and cooking utensils would be shipped once she got there.

"Don't worry about your Grandmama," Hannah repeated. "When you don't come running back after a couple of weeks like she expects you to, we'll calm her down," she said with a wink.

"Her chrysanthemums will be going like a riot in about a month and she'll be hosting the garden club," Ned added. "That'll distract her."

Brooke turned back to the brick Federalist-style mansion to see her grandmother's silhouette pull back quickly from one of the tall, multipaned windows. Her absence, Brooke knew, was calculated to deepen her granddaughter's guilt. She sighed deeply, then gave the maid and butler quick hugs. She quietly got into the little car and drove away.

Brooke had been to London and Paris, but she had never been to southeastern Oklahoma. Now, two hours from Tulsa and her grandmother, she was on the Indian Nation Turnpike bypassing towns with exotic Indian names. They were no more than pinpoints on a map.

She glanced into the rearview mirror and saw her short, tousled blond hair. Her darkly lashed green eyes appeared mildly troubled. She was headed into her future, but it seemed as if the past was never far behind. The image of the old Maple Ridge mansion, which her great-grandfather had built when he struck oil in the 1920s, seemed to flash into the silvery glass.

It was a beautiful and majestic place. Despite the September heat, a profusion of caladiums and begonias thrived in the shade of the old oaks. It was perfect in every detail, from the glossy oak floors to the imported chandeliers. It was in the city's most exclusive area, a richly preserved mausoleum from the days of quick riches in the oil fields when men like her great-

The Biggest Heart in Choctaw Hollow 7

grandfather lit cigars with ten-dollar bills. Life should have been happy for those who lived there.

For her great-grandfather, it was. But that wasn't always so for the next generation. Her grandfather did little but enjoy the fruits of his father's labor. As heir to Crosswaite Oil Company, the riches came without working for them. The tedious details of running a corporation were left to subordinates while Grandfather and Grandmama threw parties and took cruises. Grandmama, the spoiled only child of a Philadelphia banker, loved the social whirl. Grandfather, it was said, loved his Irish whiskey, but a most discreet drunk he was.

They indulged their two children, Brooke's mother Celeste, and their son, William Anthony Crosswaite III. But the family was never the same after Uncle Will's plane was shot down during the Vietnam War.

Brooke's mother tried too hard to replace her adored brother and ended up neurotic and depressed with no life outside her family and rarefied social circle. Brooke was seventeen when her mother died in a car accident that some speculated might have been a suicide. It had been only cruel gossip, Grandmama had said.

Brooke's father, Carson Adler, had taken the helm of the family business, leading to the name change—Crosswaite-Adler Oil Company. He had done everything he could to make her mother happy, including attending the social functions that he hated and enduring a job he disliked, but Celeste Crosswaite Adler could not be lifted from her melancholy.

Adler, a frustrated artist who gave Brooke her first

lessons in sketching, had died just a year ago after most of the shares of the company had been sold at a loss. For the last decade, the oil business had not been good.

Her father's death was the second blow in a year for her. While studying art in Chicago, Brooke had fallen in love with Richard Mather, a promising young MBA who worked for a national corporation. They'd met in an art gallery. Tall and dark, he showed her the city's quaint nooks and crannies. He was urbane, yet down-to-earth, sophisticated but unpretentious. He was all the things that she admired in a man. She'd taken him home to meet her father and her grandmother. She'd gone with him to his family's farm in southern Illinois. Then came the stunning revelation. A friend told her that he had been bragging that he was going to the be the next chief executive officer of Crosswaite-Adler Oil.

"What's wrong with dreaming?" he'd asked, when she questioned him about it. "You're a rich girl, Brooke. When it comes to suitors, money is always going to enter into the equation."

It wasn't that she'd never thought of that before. But the men she'd dated in the past had been the sons of people in her family's social circle. Money, it was always assumed, would marry money. But that was the world she wanted away from. And anyone outside that world could have less than honorable intentions in pursuing her. She was trapped and afraid to love again.

All Brooke knew was that she wanted out from under the burden of wealth and status. Finally, she was

The Biggest Heart in Choctaw Hollow

able to strike the agreement with her grandmother. In six years, when she was thirty, her trust fund would be parceled out to her in ten installments over ten years. But her grandmother had agreed that if she could prove within a year that she could support herself in a reasonable manner, it would be turned over to the charity of her choice and she would become an heiress without a fortune.

After stirring around Tulsa vainly searching for something in the all-too-competitive field of graphic design and also sensing that potential employers didn't think that an Adler really needed a job, she managed to find work with the Arts and Humanities Council as a circuit-riding art teacher in the remote towns in the Ouachita Mountains. She suspected she got the job because of the generous donations her family had given the organization in the past. It paid little, but she'd make it somehow. As a sign of faith and determination, she'd brought with her only enough money to live on until her first paycheck. Then if she were very lucky, perhaps she could interest a small gallery in her watercolors.

The job had been described to her as a sort of "Peace Corps" for writers, artists, and musicians. She would be assigned a cabin in Choctaw Hollow, population 2476. It was the largest of the minuscule towns in the Ouachitas. She would travel to surrounding schools on a daily basis. It had been the aspect of helping others while earning money that had given the job appeal despite its modest pay.

As the miles went by, the rolling hills of southeastern Oklahoma grew higher and the valleys deeper. The sun, which had been behind her in that peculiar, golden preautumn slant, had now disappeared behind a veil of thickening clouds. Brooke had never seen clouds quite like these. They were black and purple and as massive as the hills underneath them. They seemed to be dragging under their own weight.

A gust of wind caught her by surprise, almost swooping the little car right out from under her. She took a deep breath to steady her jumping nerves and clenched the steering wheel tightly. Suddenly, huge droplets of water began to splatter the windshield.

With little warning, the meandering highway turned into hairpin curves, curves so pronounced that they had to be taken at a crawl. As Brooke braked around the twisting asphalt, she could see plunging ravines on each side. Only low guardrails separated the pavement from the thickly wooded valleys below.

She trained her eyes carefully on the road, but the spattering drops turned into a pummeling rain which then erupted into a torrent. She switched her windshield wipers on high speed but they couldn't keep pace with the deluge. She looked frantically for a place to pull over, but she couldn't see anything except for the gray walls of water surrounding her. She slowed even more, desperately peering over the steering wheel.

The pounding of her heart seemed even louder than the windshield wipers as she struggled to maintain control. Just when the little voice deep within her heart asked, "What have you gotten yourself into?" the rain suddenly slowed enough that she could see a sign reading. CHOCTAW HOLLOW 2 MILES.

The Biggest Heart in Choctaw Hollow 11

With a sigh of relief, Brooke sped up, but not before she saw a missing chunk of asphalt a few feet in front of her. Brooke gave the steering wheel a quick twist, but it was too late. The car slipped off into the muddy ooze and slammed into the guardrail. Her head thumped against the mirror so violently that she saw stars, followed by total darkness.

"How do you feel?"

Brooke heard a masculine voice and blinked uncomprehendingly at the large but fuzzy form in front of her. She touched her fingers to a throbbing knot on the upper right side of her forehead. Her heart kicked. "What happened? Where am I?"

"You had an accident. You're in Choctaw Hollow at a medical clinic."

Brooke tried to sit up but he gently touched her shoulder and nudged her back down.

"You didn't answer my question," he said. "How do you feel?"

"I don't feel like dancing."

The shape hovering over her took on details, one being a barely perceptible smile. But the eyes, a deep gray-blue that reminded Brooke of slate after a rain, were cool and distant and studied her with a detached curiosity. His jaw was firmly set. Planted in the middle of a stubbornly crinkled chin was a dimple. A few strands of straight, thick brown hair raked boyishly across his forehead.

He stood up to full height, which appeared to be an inch or two over six feet, and paced back and forth past the foot of her cot. She guessed him to be in his early thirties. He wore a red and gray plaid shirt with sleeves rolled up to the elbows and a pair of snugly fitting faded jeans. As he strode toward her, Brooke propped herself up on her elbows. She could see that he was wearing hiking boots and thick woolen socks. He stopped a few feet away from her, crossed his arms over his chest, and studied her as if she were a puzzling abstract painting.

"Who are you?" she asked.

"Drew Griffin. I'm your doctor."

Brooke sat up with such a start that it caused an extra sharp throb in her head. "You don't look like one."

The dimple in his chin deepened in apparent consternation. Ignoring her comment, he plucked a pillow from a nearby cabinet, plumped it and placed it behind her other one. "Sit up if you like, but keep as still as possible." Without another word, he left the room.

As soon as the door clicked behind him, Brooke gingerly sneaked out of bed. Her blue cotton jumper was rumpled, the front spotted with blood. She felt a pull on her leg and lifted her hem to find a small bandage covering her knee. She examined the rest of her legs, checked her elbows, then ran her hands over her face. The damage, she concluded with relief, seemed limited. Yet she felt a growing soreness as she walked toward the room's single window. She looked outside to find Mattie's Quilt Shop. Next door was the Green Tomato Café.

As Brooke groped to put everything together, the door suddenly opened and Drew Griffin reappeared. This time, he wore a white laboratory coat over his

The Biggest Heart in Choctaw Hollow 13

jeans. A stethoscope was slung casually over his broad shoulders and in his left hand was a clipboard. He looked at her disapprovingly.

"You were to keep still." His tone was firm.

Brooke crossed her hands defensively over her chest. "I can't. I have too much to do."

He took her gently but firmly by the arm and led her back to the cot. "Your car slid off the road; a passing motorist found you unconscious. You were brought here by ambulance. You've had a rough day, Miss Adler. Whatever you have to do is going to have to wait because I'm keeping you overnight for observation."

"How do you know my name?" she countered.

"The police checked your identification and before you ask, your car has been moved to a safe place—Frank Harjo's Garage and Salvage."

"But I have to contact the school," she protested, explaining why she'd come to Choctaw Hollow.

"I'll contact whomever you want," he said, "but in the meantime, lie down and rest. Doctor's orders."

Brooke grudgingly got in bed. "Your bedside manner leaves something to be desired."

His full bottom lip twitched slightly, but he said nothing.

"At least tell me why I should be under observation," she said.

He took a penlight from his pocket and tilted her chin upwards. The heat of his fingers burned her skin. He lifted each of her eyelids and shined the light in her eyes. "Because," he said, his handsome mouth startlingly close, "with an injury like this, you could develop symptoms—dizziness, slow respiration, nausea, unconsciousness—that signal a concussion."

Brooke collapsed back on the pillow. Suddenly, the weight of the day's events seemed crushing. She'd started out so strong and confident. Now here she sat with a huge bump on her head and a wrecked car. She resisted the urge to cry. She let out a deep sigh instead. How could everything have gone so wrong so soon?

The doctor made some notes on the clipboard, then put the stethoscope in his ears. Brooke followed his instructions to breathe deeply as he pressed the cold instrument to her body. His touch brought an unwanted flicker of warmth that left her surprised.

"You're probably going to be fine," he said, seemingly avoiding her eyes. He made a few more marks on the clipboard. There was a brief pause. "Brooke Crosswaite Adler. Is that as in Crosswaite-Adler Oil?"

Brooke cringed slightly. "Yes."

His chin crinkled slightly. "I'm afraid you may be out of your element here."

"What do you mean?" she asked.

"The beauty of these mountains is deceiving. This is rough country. It's for the callused and those accustomed to hardship. It's not a place for city girls, rich city girls in particular."

He stuffed the stethoscope into a pocket and stood. "Stay in bed for the rest of the afternoon, and don't be traipsing about."

He shot her a look of disapproval, then left the room.

Chapter Two

As soon as the door clicked shut, Brooke scrambled out of bed again and began to pace the floor. Rest? How could she when her own doctor intimated that she should promptly pack up and go home?

She paced a while longer, then watched the comings and goings along Main Street. Old men chatted on benches and people waved at each other as they ran their errands. Then, as dusk approached, almost everyone seemed to disappear.

She sat on the bed with a thud. Could this all be a bad dream? The sudden squall of a baby made it clear that everything was all too real.

As the baby's cries dwindled to soft hiccups, she could hear Dr. Griffin's rich baritone in one of the adjoining rooms.

Brooke padded to the bathroom, feeling aches and bruises that didn't seem to be there before, and bathed her face in cold water. The bandage on her forehead caused her bangs to stick straight out. Her skin was pale. Her clothes needed changing and there was no sign of her luggage. The only thing about her that didn't seem to be askew was the elegant little gold necklace at her throat. If she knew, Grandmama would be hysterical. She combed her hair quickly, smoothed down her clothing the best she could, and discreetly opened the door.

She found herself in a hallway leading to the waiting room. She could see several rows of what appeared to be church pews. On the wall were large Norman Rockwell prints, all with medical themes. The air smelled of antiseptic and bubble gum.

Suddenly, a tall, tired-looking woman appeared in the waiting area. A thin baby with a shock of wispy blond hair fretted against her shoulder. Brooke retreated into the shadows of the hallway.

"You were wise to bring him in, Lois." Brooke heard the doctor's voice but she couldn't see him. "High fever in an infant can be dangerous. He should be fine, but call me if there's a problem."

"Thank you, doctor," she said. "A... about the bill. My husband has been laid off. If you need your office cleaned again—"

"It's all right," he said. "Don't worry about it now."

After Drew accompanied the woman outside, Brooke stepped into the waiting room. When he returned, his eyes met hers in a flash of surprise. It was quickly taken over by professional reserve. "How do

The Biggest Heart in Choctaw Hollow 17

you feel? Are you experiencing any drowsiness, nausea, or other symptoms?"

"No, but my stomach is growling."

"Sorry," he said, pulling the stethoscope from around his neck and sticking it into his coat pocket. "I'll run over to the café and get you something."

"What about yourself?" she asked. "Have you eaten?"

His mouth quirked slightly. "Not since breakfast."

"You should take better care of yourself."

"My job is taking care of others," he said matter-of-factly. "What would you like from the café?"

Brooke twisted her gold necklace in contemplation. "Grilled chicken with sautéed vegetables would be nice."

He looked at her with disdain. "They don't do nouvelle cuisine at the Green Tomato Café."

Brooke crossed her arms defensively over her chest. "That's not nouvelle cuisine. That's just—food."

His jaw was firm, yet there was a flicker of amusement in his eyes. "Let me put Choctaw Hollow into culinary perspective. A lot of people here practically live on pinto beans and salt pork. To them, that's just food. In the summer they have gardens, and if they're lucky, they'll have chicken on Sundays. Fried chicken. To them, there's no other kind.

"While you're here, think plain, not fancy. And plain can be pretty darned good. I can recommend the Green Tomato's chicken-fried steak, mashed potatoes, fried okra, and pinto beans. Gertie whips up an exquisite cream gravy."

Brooke's cheeks tingled. "Does the steak have to be chicken-fried?"

"What are you thinking about instead—steak au poivre?"

"Well..." Brooke threw out her hands in exasperation. "That might be better. It's just steak with cracked peppercorns. That's not too fancy and besides, it would have fewer calories."

He shook his head ruefully. "It's not worth getting Gertie upset over a few calories. She can be very temperamental. I am prescribing a chicken-fried steak. It will do you good."

Brooke looked into his uncompromising blue-gray gaze and gave a sigh of resignation. "I'll set the table, that is, if you happen to have one."

He pointed to a door off the waiting room. "My living quarters are in there. The kitchen is in the back."

After he left, Brooke opened the door marked "private" and found herself inside a small, but surprisingly comfortable-looking room with a plump chintz-covered sofa and matching armchair. A large rag rug was centered over the polished oak floor. A built-in bookcase filled with medical books occupied one wall. In front of it was a rocking chair and a floor lamp. Magazines and open books were strewn about the floor and across a small pine table at the end of the room. All of it gave off a sense of cozy disarray.

But the kitchen was a different matter. It was tiny, barely big enough to hold the essential appliances and a basic set of cabinets. The sink was piled with dishes—all dirty. There was no dishwasher. Brooke opened the cabinet and found two clean but mismatched plates, one with a stalk of wheat in the center and another with a chipped floral design. In the silverware drawer, she found equally mismatched pieces of flatware.

When she cleared the books and magazines off the table, their outlines remained in the dust. She quickly wiped it down and arranged the plates. She glanced about the room for anything that might serve as a centerpiece, but all she could find was a drooping philodendron on a window sill. In the kitchen, she watered it and found a pair of scissors. She folded a white paper napkin and made a few cutouts. Unfolded, it resembled a doily which she placed on the center of the table. She positioned the plant on top.

Then she sat on the sofa and thought about the puzzling man who lived there. The thick wall of formality he'd built between them seemed to go beyond the doctor-patient relationship. She sensed that he was wary of her. Once men discovered she was an Adler, they tended to be altogether too friendly. But that didn't seem to impress Drew Griffin. That should have made her happy, but for some inexplicable reason, it didn't.

He returned with two plastic foam boxes and a bottle of wine.

"The preferred local drink with chicken-fried steak is heavily sweetened iced tea, but I thought you might prefer the wine," he said, presenting her with the bottle. "I don't want to be remembered as a completely inept host."

"Thank you," she said. "It was very thoughtful of you."

He responded with a half grin and Brooke realized that it was the first time she'd seen him smile. "I hope you don't mind drinking it out of a jelly glass," he said.

"Not at all."

A moment later, he emerged from the kitchen with the glasses. He opened the bottle with a loud pop of the cork and poured a small amount in each glass. Then he transferred the contents of the cartons to their plates. "Nice touch," he said wryly, pointing to the makeshift centerpiece. "I might have known."

For a few moments, they ate in awkward silence. Brooke couldn't deny that she felt out of place, but in time, that would change, she told herself.

The food was hearty and delicious. Brooke hadn't realized she was so hungry. "I must send Gertie a card. She's a wonderful cook."

He studied her with a mocking light in his eyes. "It would probably be the first time that she's been complimented on hand-engraved vellum."

Brooke laid down her fork and frowned. "I didn't happen to bring any hand-engraved vellum with me, Dr. Griffin."

"You can call me Drew," he offered.

"You're skirting around the subject, Drew," she said, placing emphasis on his name. "What makes you think I'm some sort of dissident debutante?"

He pushed his empty plate away and leaned forward on his elbows. An errant strand of hair fell across his brow. "Because that's what you are."

Brooke leaned back and glared at him in heated silence.

"There have been various sorts of do-gooders come through here thinking they're going to civilize the natives, to make this a better place," he continued. "Well, the natives are already much more civilized than people are in most cities, and as for making this a better place—some people like things the way they are."

"Are you one of them?" she asked.

He shook his head slowly. "There's plenty of room for improvement. The most important thing is how you approach people. They're sensitive. They don't want to be patronized."

Brooke's cheeks grew warm. "What makes you think I would do that?"

He studied her carefully. "I don't think you would on purpose. But here you sit with a bandage on your forehead and wrinkles in your clothing and you've still got wealth and breeding written all over you. You're not one of them, Brooke. They will wonder, as I do, what brings you here."

Brooke picked up her fork and studied the bent tines.

"I hope you're not contemplating using that on me," he said.

She shot him a look of annoyance, then laid the fork down. "I'm here to introduce children to art while I do some painting of my own. You already know that."

He toyed with the rim of his glass. "I do," he said, glancing up. "But sometimes, people also come to the mountains to escape something or to search for themselves."

Brooke stiffened. Then she looked directly into his gaze. "What brings you here?"

A hint of amusement played across his face. "A fair question. I'm in my second year of a four-year service program. By practicing in a medically underserved area, I can erase my debts from medical school. I know what it's like to grow up in this area, Brooke, because I did. My father died when I was young and my mother barely supported us by working in a shirt factory. It took me five years to get through college because I worked my way through as a full-time hospital orderly.

"Choctaw Hollow had been looking for a doctor for years after old Doc Murphy died, so when I came along, they were beside themselves. The town rents this space for me. A group of women got together and fixed it up. I feel I owe these people something. They need me, and even if I didn't need them, I'd probably be here anyway."

He got up and took a few steps toward her. He touched her lightly on the shoulder, sending an unexpected flutter of warmth through her. "Come in the examination room. Let me take another look at that bump."

She followed him to a small room off the waiting room. He hit a switch, quickly flooding the room with light. As she sat on the end of the examining table, he gently lifted the bandage off. Brooke stole a look at him as he concentrated on the wound. There were shadows of fatigue under his eyes. A day's growth of beard shadowed his cheeks. His hair was tousled, his

The Biggest Heart in Choctaw Hollow 23

clothing rumpled. Yet from all that emerged a refined sensuality that Brooke couldn't ignore.

"It's turning a lovely shade of purple," he said, tilting her face upward, "but that's normal. Within a week, you'll barely notice it."

He replaced the bandage and considering his hands were large and strong, his touch was surprisingly gentle. He stepped back, folded his arms across his chest and studied her critically. "Brooke, this rugged place is no match for you."

She bristled. "What are you saying, that I should go back to the Junior Charity League, where I belong?"

"Why make life hard for yourself?" he countered.

She scooted off the table and faced him squarely. "Because I made an agreement with my grandmother," she said, filling in the details. "It may surprise you to know that being rich isn't all it's cracked up to be."

There was a mocking glint in his eyes. "Then maybe you're right to come here. These mountains will give you perspective. But let me offer you some of my own. You're an orchid among rough and tangled underbrush. The stores here, Brooke, don't stock Perrier or Swiss chocolate. I predict you won't last a month."

Her cheeks flamed in anger. "I predict, Drew Griffin, that you'll be taking back every word you said and then some."

A barely perceptible smile showed he was unconvinced.

"Good night, doctor," she said, twisting her gold locket, and strode angrily out of the room.

When Brooke awoke the next morning, the luggage from the trunk of the Miata was sitting inside her door. On the table beside her bed was a plate with two doughnuts and a glass of milk. Underneath the glass was a note written in a bold scrawl.

Sorry, but this was the closest I could get to croissants.
—*Drew*
P.S. I'll be your chauffeur for a while. It doesn't look like you'll be getting your car back anytime soon.

Her stomach tightened. She nibbled at a doughnut, but tasted nothing. She stewed for a moment about the car, but what concerned her most was that now there were two people who didn't think she'd succeed, Grandmama and Drew.

Grandmama she understood, but not Drew. Just when she would conclude he was hopelessly exasperating, he'd do something thoroughly decent and thoughtful. Perhaps he felt guilty. Maybe he was just carrying out the Hippocratic oath. Didn't it say something like "do no harm"? Anyway, she was certain of one thing. He wasn't offering to drive her around because he liked her. He'd already made it clear that she belonged back in her grandmother's Maple Ridge mansion.

After she finished her breakfast, she indulged in a

hot and leisurely shower. She shampooed her hair, wincing as the soap stung the abrasion on her forehead. She blew her hair back into its usual natural, straight style, then put on a loosely constructed blue linen dress. She lightly applied makeup. She planned to meet the county superintendent today. She wanted to look reasonably professional.

She sighed deeply. Everything would work out. She'd get settled into her cabin, away from Drew Griffin and his impossible attitude, and her car would be in working order, no doubt, within a week. She'd lose herself in her work, organizing art classes, and finding lovely mountain spots to watercolor. Grandmama would become immersed in the social activities of the fall and forget all about her and her imaginary ills and before Brooke would know it, the year would be over. She could already feel her spirits rise.

The waiting room was strangely empty although it was past nine o'clock. Brooke listened for the sound of Drew's voice but there was only silence. Timidly, she knocked on the door of his living quarters. After a moment, the lock turned and the door opened. Drew, shirtless and with a towel around his neck, appeared. His face was covered with shaving lather and a razor was poised in one hand. Her eyes locked onto his in surprise.

"I'm sorry," she murmured, "I..."

"Please excuse my appearance," he said. "If I'd known you were coming, I would have put on a tuxedo."

"I'm sure you have dozens of them," she said, her voice spiked with sarcasm.

He crimped a corner of his mouth. The mask of lather brought out the shimmer in his eyes. As he wiped an errant bit of suds from his shoulder, she couldn't help but notice the muscular planes of his chest. They were covered with a film of dark, curling hair. Unaccustomed to the sight of so much masculinity, she took an awkward step backwards. "I'll wait for you out here," she said.

"As you wish," he said, the corners of his eyes crinkling.

Brooke fidgeted in the waiting room, leafing through a copy of *Country Decorating*, but she couldn't concentrate. There was nothing in her upbringing to prepare her for a man like Drew Griffin. When he wasn't being distant, he was insolent and downright irreverent.

The door clicked open and she jumped up. Drew, dressed in his customary jeans and hiking boots and a blue plaid shirt, appeared. "Where would you like to go first?" His tone had reverted back to a stiff formality.

"Please, I could walk, if you'll just point the way," she argued. "You must have patients to see this morning."

He shook his head. "I'm off on Wednesdays unless there's an emergency." He pointed to the pager attached to his belt. "I can be always be reached if necessary. Besides," he said, looking at her Italian-made pumps, "I wouldn't call those walking shoes."

"They have flat heels," she countered.

He responded with a chiding look. "Let's go."

She followed him outside, where a mud-spattered

The Biggest Heart in Choctaw Hollow 27

dark blue Jeep Cherokee sat parked. He opened the door for her and shifted a medical bag from the passenger seat to the back. "I explained everything to the superintendent. He's expecting us."

"Thank you," she said, getting inside.

He slid behind the wheel. "How's the head this morning?" he asked, turning toward her.

"Much better," she said. "Grandmama always said my head was exceptionally hard."

His eyes flicked devilishly over her face. He didn't need words to say he agreed.

Reginald Krauthammer, superintendent of the Choctaw County Schools, was a rotund, red-faced man with a booming voice and a hearty laugh.

"Mighty glad to have you here," he said, pumping Brooke's hand vigorously. "Awful sorry about your accident. Unfortunately, bits of pavement tend to slide off into the canyon when it rains. We all have to be real careful around here, even those of us driving these roads all our lives. Drew can tell you that."

Drew nodded.

"We're awful proud of this boy here," Mr. Krauthammer said. "He's one of our own. We think the world of him."

Drew responded with an embarrassed shrug.

Mr. Krauthammer led them to his secretary, who supplied Brooke with maps of the area and schedules for art classes in the five schools in which she would be working.

"And of course, one of the perks with this job is a cabin out on the edge of town. Offers a nice view of the mountains and sits on the edge of a creek. It's nothing fancy, but the art types in the past have liked it. You pay only one hundred fifty dollars a month." He held up the keys. "It's all yours."

After Brooke paid the first month's rent, they went to Frank Harjo's Garage and Salvage where Frank, a plump Choctaw Indian, greeted Drew with a playful punch on the shoulder.

"This is Brooke Adler, the owner of the red Miata convertible," Drew explained.

Frank nodded in greeting while wiping the grease from his hands. "I just gave it a goin' over. It doesn't look so good."

Her heart sank. "What do you mean?"

He strolled over to the little car, gesturing at the right front side. The fender was mangled and the front wheel was grotesquely twisted. "What we have here is a broken axle and some front-end problems. "We're lookin' at about one thousand dollars worth of work."

Brooke's stomach churned. In an effort to economize, she'd raised the deductible on her insurance to one thousand dollars. That was more money than she had brought with her. And because of the agreement, asking Grandmama for help was out of the question. "I'm low on cash right now and it will be a month before I get paid," she said, her voice weak. "Could you give some time to pay it out?"

The man's eyes widened in surprise. "Well, I suppose so." Then he paused. "I'll tell you what. I know you're going to be needin' this car as soon as possible, so I'll go ahead and get started on it. It'll probably take me about two weeks though, maybe three. For two hundred dollars, you can get it out, then pay out the rest.''

She took her first breath in several seconds. ''That's very nice of you. Do you know how I might get something to drive in the meantime?''

''I'll get you something cheap to rent. Don't worry,'' he said.

''One thousand dollars,'' Brooke muttered as they drove toward the cabin.

''It's only money,'' Drew said wryly. ''Your grandmother probably spends that on caviar.''

She shot him a scolding look. ''This has to do with me, not Grandmama. This is money I have to scrape up myself. On top of that I have to eat, pay the rent, and buy art supplies.''

''Welcome to the real world,'' he said with a glint of amusement on his face.

Miffed, Brooke gave him an unappreciative glance out of the corner of her eye. She couldn't help but notice that he had a handsome profile. It was a shame that such good looks had to be wasted on such a disagreeable man.

They stopped at the clinic to pick up her luggage, then made the rest of the ten-minute drive in relative silence. Despite her anxiety about the future, Brooke couldn't help but notice the beauty of the heavily forested countryside. Cattle grazed in the clearings.

Drew turned down a gravel road and stopped in front of a small log cabin shaded by a large oak tree. Even close-up, the cabin looked very small.

He stopped the Jeep and took the cabin keys from

her. As they walked to the porch, mud oozed over her pumps. She wrinkled her nose as she took them off and left them by the door.

"It's part of country living," he said. "Get used to it."

The cabin had four rooms, counting the bathroom and a kitchen that someone had already stocked with food. It was scrubbed clean, yet the furniture was worn and sparse. The bed sagged slightly in the middle. But the living room had a large fireplace and a bank of north windows that offered plenty of steady light for painting and a lovely view of the mountains.

Drew plumped a pillow on the sofa and dust motes rose in the air. "It's not Aspen, but you'll be living better than many in these mountains."

Brooke nodded bravely. The mustiness threatened to make her sneeze. "It just needs a woman's touch," she said, her voice tight.

Drew brought in her luggage, then lingered awkwardly in the door. His body almost filled the doorway. "Jessie Johnico lives just up the road with her grandson, so you won't be totally alone." He handed her a business card. I'm as close as the telephone. Call or page me. Before I go, is there anything else you need?"

Before she could answer, a clap of thunder rattled the windows, sending her heart to her throat. A downpour followed, pummeling the roof noisily. "Don't worry, I'll be fine," she said. "I'll be settled in no time."

"Don't hesitate to call me," he repeated. His voice

was stern, but his eyes, for a fleeting moment, lost their customary look of detachment.

"Thank you for everything you've done. I'm sorry to have been so much trouble."

"A patient is never trouble," he said.

Brooke watched discreetly from the window as he drove away. Then an odd emptiness enveloped her, leaving her disoriented. She picked up a throw pillow, hugged it to her chest, then promptly sneezed. She sneezed again, then again. Then she heard a plopping sound. She followed it to the bedroom, where a wet spot was forming on the center of the bed. She looked up to find a leak in the roof.

She blinked, hoping it had been an illusion, but the drip came even faster. She sneezed again. She thought of her car and the one thousand dollars she couldn't afford and sneezed twice more.

Things weren't going well at all.

Chapter Three

Once she came to her senses, Brooke dashed into the kitchen and threw open cabinets until she found a saucepan. She raced back into the bedroom and planted it in the middle of the bed.

With chagrin, she sat on the edge of the mattress and watched the pot slowly fill up.

What had begun as a downpour slowed to a steady patter on the roof. The cracks of thunder had dwindled to a low rumble, but that failed to brighten her spirits. Suddenly, having to endure Drew's disdain of her background seemed better than having no one around at all.

She sat up straight, forcing herself to be optimistic. Maybe she wasn't used to roughing it. At home, Hannah would bring her breakfast in bed if she asked for it. But the price was too high. Going home meant the manipulations of Grandmama, the meaningless social whirl, and the men who would use her to reach their ambitions. She could not and would not go home.

She jumped up and gave the bed a hard yank away from the leak and positioned the pan on the floor underneath the steady drip. She dragged her large, heavy suitcases into the bedroom and began to unpack. The silk dresses and crisp linen pants seemed oddly out of place against the roughly chinked logs. She owned one pair of jeans, of which Grandmama soundly disapproved, and an oversize black sweatshirt on which "Paris" was written in large white letters. It wasn't a favorite of Grandmama's either. She slipped out of her linen dress and put on both.

She emptied the saucepan into the bathroom sink, then suddenly realized she was hungry. She returned the pan to the bedroom then looked inside the refrigerator. To her surprise, it was stocked with fresh fruit and sandwich ingredients. In the freezer were frozen entrées. She selected lasagna and popped it unto the ancient electric oven. The door closed with a creak.

Just as she sat down on the musty old sofa to wait for her food to warm, the telephone rang. She jumped to answer it. It was Grandmama.

"Brooke, I've been frantic." Her voice was pitched high with excitement. "I'm hyperventilating. Why haven't you called?"

Brooke felt a twinge of guilt. "Grandmama, I'm sorry," she said, "but things just got hectic. I was going to call you within the hour."

"What do you mean—'hectic'?" she asked. "Something's wrong, isn't it? Tell me about it at once."

"Nothing is wrong, Grandmama. I've been busy

meeting the people of Choctaw Hollow and getting settled," she said, carefully sidestepping the accident.

"Thank goodness I was able to track you down through that Mr. Krauthandler before I started hyperventilating. You know that's terrible for my heart."

"Grandmama, it's Krauthammer, and yes, I know about your heart and I'm very sorry. But remember, I simply said I'd let you know if there were any problems. If not, I'd get in touch with you in a few days. I'm fine. I really am."

"What is the cabin like? Does it have good amenities? What about central heating? I don't want you to catch cold. And what about your allergies?"

"It's just a cabin, Grandmama. I'm perfectly comfortable," she said, stretching the truth from Oklahoma to Afghanistan.

"Perhaps a hotel would be more suitable, something with good room service."

Brooke sighed in exasperation. "Grandmama, there are no hotels like that here."

"You won't be happy there, dear. You'll see," the old lady responded. "You'll come back to the wonderful life I've given you here. And my health failing though it is, I will be waiting with open arms."

What was left of the bump on Brooke's head began to throb. "Grandmama, I'll call you in a few days. In the meantime, don't you have a garden club meeting to worry about?"

"Yes, on top of having a runaway granddaughter."

"I have not run away. Now, please . . ."

"It's probably best for my heart that I hang up now," she said. "Now, why can't you be more like

The Biggest Heart in Choctaw Hollow 35

your mother was?" she said, asking the familiar rhetorical question. "Good night, dear."

"Good night, Grandmama." She hung up and took a deep, shuddering breath.

Suddenly, she smelled food burning. She rushed to the oven to find the lasagna nicely charred around the edges. With a groan, she set it on top the stove to cool, then set a single place at the little Formica and metal dinette by the window. She poured herself a glass of milk and got a mystery novel from the suitcase. While in the bedroom, she emptied the saucepan again. The dripping, thankfully, had stopped.

She tried to read as she ate, but she had trouble concentrating. The lasagna was bland and lukewarm in the middle. She thought longingly of Hannah's lasagna with three cheeses and a sauce of imported plum tomatoes. Then she took another bite of the frozen fare and chewed determinedly.

She was nibbling on a dessert of grapes and a sliced peach when she first sensed something—a presence of some sort. She put her food down and listened. There was a slight rustle. Brooke, unaccustomed to country noises, told herself it was a squirrel or a raccoon. She continued to eat. Then she heard a metallic pop that seemed to come from just outside the window. She jumped up. Tiny bumps tingled along her arms as she backed away from the uncurtained window.

The sensation of something, or someone, nearby heightened, as she continued to back away at an angle, keeping as much out of view as she could while watching the window. Suddenly, what appeared to be a human silhouette popped up above the windowsill, then back down again.

She jumped back, her heart thrashing wildly. Her mind racing, she instinctively grabbed a heavy skillet with a long handle. Before she got halfway across the living room to call the sheriff, there was a thump, followed by a clatter. Next came what sounded like the cry of a child.

Wielding the skillet, Brook ran outside to the kitchen window just in time to find a small form running into the night. Just underneath the window was an overturned bucket.

"Thaney!" a female voice called. "You get home this minute!"

Brooke, her heart fluttering, followed the fleeing form to the road beside the cabin. In the light of a roadside lamp, she could see a waiting adult with her hands on her hips.

"Has he been bothering you?" the woman called.

Brooke, breathless and feeling suddenly silly packing a cast-iron skillet, gave a laugh of nervous relief. Her wobbling knees barely held her up. "He was peeping in the window. He gave me a little scare, that's all."

She looked down to find a dark-haired boy of about seven standing partially behind the woman as if he were using her as a shield. The woman took the boy by the shoulders and positioned him in front of her. "What have you been up to now?" she asked.

"I just wanted to see who was in there," he said, pointing to the cabin.

The woman, bespectacled, middle-aged and with the

dark coloring and cheekbones of the Choctaws, frowned. "It's not nice to go peeping in people's houses. Now tell the young lady you're sorry."

The boy studied his muddy sneakers. "I'm sorry," he said without looking up.

Brooke bent over and tilted his chin upward. "Your apology is accepted."

She held out her hand to the woman. "I'm Brooke Adler."

The woman smiled shyly. "I'm Jessie Johnico. I live just up the road. Thaney is my grandson."

"I'm pleased to meet you both. I'm new here in Choctaw Hollow."

"I can tell you're not from around here," Jessie said.

Brooke swallowed hard. She didn't want to be that conspicuous. "The mountains are really beautiful," she said, dodging Jessie's assessment.

The woman nodded. "But the rains have been a problem this summer," she said. "The old folks say they can't ever remember such a wet year. The mountain roads are crumbling and the creeks are nearly over their banks. And the rain keeps coming. The loggers are having trouble harvesting the trees, some are getting laid off, and on top of that, all this flooding has damaged acres and acres of seedlings."

"That's too bad," Brooke said, regretting the inadequacy of her response. It made her realize again what an outsider she was.

When she returned to the cabin, the telephone was ringing. Grandmama again? Despite the doctor's assurances that the old lady's only serious malady was hypochondria, Brooke still worried. What was imagined had been known to become real. She quickly snatched the receiver off the hook.

"I was afraid you'd been eaten by a bear."

Her heart skittered at the sound of Drew's voice. "I was outside talking to Jessie Johnico and her grandson," she said defensively. Then, a twinge of realization darted through her. "Are there really bears out here?"

"Lots of them," he said, his tone light.

Brooke was not amused. "Why didn't you tell me?"

"I didn't think of it. Besides, you've told me most assuredly that you're quite capable of taking care of yourself."

"If you believe that, why did you call?" she asked, miffed.

"I'm making my evening rounds, so to speak. How's your head?"

Brooke touched her forehead. "It's still attached to the rest of me."

"Is everything okay at the cabin?"

Craning her neck, Brooke looked in the bedroom where the pan sat. "Moist, but otherwise fine," she said obliquely.

"Brooke, Frank Harjo has located a car for you. He got it through a fellow mechanic for fifty dollars a week. Does that seem fair?"

"Oh, yes," she said with a tone of confidence, unsure of what it really cost to rent a car.

The Biggest Heart in Choctaw Hollow 39

"Good. I'll pick you up around eight in the morning and you can get it."

"It's very kind of you."

"A thank-you note won't be necessary."

She sighed in exasperation. "Drew Griffin, honestly. I'm an Adler, not an Astor, and a renegade Adler at that. I'm a woman like any other."

"I hadn't noticed."

"It's time you did. I can take care of myself quite well, thank you."

After she hung up, she had several troubling thoughts. One was that she wished that Drew Griffin would take her seriously. What specifically troubled her was that she cared at all how he took her. He was insolent and irreverent, even though he managed both with a maddeningly light touch. But the most troubling thought of all had to do with money. That was a worry she'd never had before.

She raced into the bedroom and grabbed her small, but expensive, leather purse. She emptied its contents on the wet bed and found fifty dollars in cash and seven hundred dollars in traveler's checks. With relatively low rent to pay, she figured it would be more than adequate until her first paycheck. It was all money she'd earned as a freelancer creating logos and designing letterheads for businesses. She'd insisted on using her own earnings to get started in Choctaw Hollow. She wanted no help from Grandmama.

The amount seemed adequate at the time. After all, she would only need food, rent, gasoline, and a few art supplies. In a demonstration of her financial independence, she'd left her credit cards on Grandmama's antique secretary. But what she didn't count on were car repair expenses, medical bills, and car rental fees. She'd only been in Choctaw Hollow two days and she was already in the red. She looked at the money in dismay. How was she going to pay all those bills and manage to eat at the same time?

She paced back and forth across the cabin's little living room. She'd have to get a temporary part-time job.

The next morning, it began to rain again. Brooke remembered the bucket that Thaney had stood on to peer into the kitchen window and stuck it under the leak. She'd tell Mr. Krauthammer about it this morning.

Brooke, wearing a black and white print cotton jumper, a white T-shirt, and a bright yellow rain slicker, stood on the front porch of the cabin listening to the steady rhythm of the rain. Low visibility had reduced the mountains to little more than dark shapes in the distance. The creek within a hundred yards of the cabin swelled.

The flash of car lights appeared over the rise leading to the cabin. Brooke recognized the Jeep, picked up her leather briefcase, and stepped to the edge of the porch.

Drew stopped in front of the cabin and got out. His jaw was firmly set but his eyes flashed with interest. "Your chariot awaits."

"A simple 'good morning' will do," she said as he opened the door for her.

He slid behind the wheel and studied her for a moment with one brow cocked. He rested his arm on the back of the seat. His fingers were within touching distance of her shoulder. His hair was slightly damp, his face rosy and freshly shaven. Her pulse quickened.

"You seem to have survived the night very well," he said.

"Disappointed?" she asked wryly.

"Of course not. A bit surprised, maybe."

She shot him a look of indignation. "You can put your crystal ball away. I'll be here tonight, the next night, and the night after that."

"What about the next night?"

"I'm not going anywhere," she bristled. "I'll be here until May."

He brushed her bangs back and inspected her forehead so closely that his lips were within inches of her face. His closeness sent sparks of sexual awareness through her.

"It's healing nicely. You won't need me anymore," he said, edging away from her.

"I'm glad you're finally acknowledging that," she said. "Except for medical emergencies, you'll see that I can make it fine without you. Thank you for your expert care. I'm sure you won't forget to send me a bill."

He grinned crookedly. "I only forget when people can't afford to pay."

He backed the Jeep out of the driveway, then drove briskly to the pavement. They rode to town in silence except for the intermittent swishing of the windshield wipers.

The main street of Choctaw Hollow was two blocks long. There was no traffic light, nor was one needed.

There was a five-and-dime, a general store, a hardware store, a bank, and all the other basics of small-town life. In Choctaw Hollow, it seemed, time had stopped thirty years ago.

Drew drove just past the edge of the business district to Frank Harjo's garage, where Frank was sitting on the bumper of a dented white pickup truck while drinking from a coffee mug. He rose as Drew brought the Jeep to a halt.

"Got her all fixed up. Here's your truck," he proclaimed proudly.

Brooke's eyes widened. She opened her mouth, but nothing came out.

"It belongs to an old friend of mine," the mechanic continued. "He fixed it up to sell, but you can use it in the meantime. It's a solid piece of machinery—in tip-top order."

Drew bit his bottom lip. "I don't know if she can manage that, Frank."

Brooke blanched at the suggestion. "Of course I can."

Drew cast her a skeptical look as she held out an open palm. Frank dropped the keys into it. She might not have driven anything that big before, but she was grateful it was cheap.

"I should get to the office then," Drew said.

Brooke thanked him, but the parting was bittersweet. As she watched the Jeep disappear around the corner, she felt suddenly like a five-year-old left at the kindergarten door on the first day of school. And that wasn't the worst of it. It wasn't just his direction that she missed. It was him.

The Biggest Heart in Choctaw Hollow 43

Well, no matter. Choctaw Hollow was a small town, too small for him not to see that she'd prove him wrong in every way. She'd turn all his doubts inside out and show him that she could manage without his help or anyone else's.

She paid Frank one hundred and fifty dollars for three weeks' use of the truck, then got inside. The steering wheel seemed as big as a bus's. She turned the key and the pickup rattled to a start. She put on a brave smile, gave the mechanic a wave and ground the gears into reverse, thankful that a high school boyfriend had taught her how to drive a manual transmission using his Alfa Romeo. She backed out of the garage and chugged toward the school.

Her first order of business was to inform Mr. Krauthammer that the cabin roof needed immediate attention. Then she made a quick inventory of the art supplies at the elementary school where she would conduct her first class on Monday. There was little, but they'd make do until she could order more finger paints, crayons, and colored chalk.

Although she was trained as an artist, not a teacher, the smell of the school invigorated her. It was the smell of books and fresh ink. It was the scent of education, which for some children would be a ticket out of the mountains.

When she finished, she went downtown and picked up a copy of the *Choctaw Hollow Bugle,* a smudgy tabloid listing everything from the number of logs hauled out of the area to who visited whom.

She sat on a sidewalk bench and turned to the want ads. She was now down to four hundred and fifty dollars and would need half that to get her car out. It was doubtful she could make it last until payday.

When it came to jobs, pickings were slim. She couldn't weld nor drill a well, nor could she work full-time. Then an advertisement for an office job caught her eye: "Needed: Part-time Girl Friday, Typing, filing, simple bookkeeping as well as some tidying up. Apply at 208 E. Main."

Brooke circled the ad boldly and jumped up, taking notice of the numbers on the storefronts. She crossed the street and followed them to the beginning of the next block. When she spotted 208, her stomach flipped with dismay. Two hundred eight was the office of Drew K. Griffin, M.D.

Chapter Four

For a moment, Brooke's feet seemed to be stuck to the sidewalk. Ask Drew Griffin for a job? Her cheeks warmed at the thought. If he wasn't thoroughly convinced that she was a pampered heiress out of her element, he would be then. He'd also have her pegged as one who didn't know the value of a dollar, who couldn't manage on an ordinary budget. It wasn't as if she could work elsewhere in Choctaw Hollow and keep it a secret. The town was too small for that. But at least she wouldn't have to see the little mocking lights that danced in his eyes.

Just as she turned to leave, the door clicked open. She glanced over her shoulder, then froze as her eyes locked onto Drew's.

"What a surprise," she said, turning toward him. "I . . . I was just out taking care of some things." She attempted a smile of composure, but inside, her wits, despite hours of social training at the knee of Grandmama, were in disarray. "I'm sorry. I've forgotten to say 'hello,' haven't I?"

He smiled crookedly. "Good morning, Brooke. Looking for something in the want ads?"

Her heart thumped against her ribs as she looked in horror at the newspaper clutched tightly against her chest. "Oh, nothing terribly extraordinary," she answered with a shrug.

His chin crinkled. "That looks like my ad there that you've got circled."

She winced at the loop of red ink. "I didn't realize at first..."

He looked at her with a directness that seemed to reach right into her mind. "I was just on my way over to the Green Tomato for a bit of lunch. Come and join me and you can explain it over the daily special—meat loaf and collard greens."

She glanced at the clean, angular line of his jaw, the tawny hint of summer sun on his skin, and the disarmingly rumpled appearance he presented. His pale blue denim shirt was rolled up at the elbows, revealing tanned, muscular forearms. Knotted loosely at his unbuttoned collar was a tie sprinkled with cartoon drawings of animals. He wore khakis and, instead of his customary hiking boots, a worn pair of loafers. The sun, which had made its first appearance since Brooke arrived, brought out dark gold highlights in his hair. Brooke swallowed hard. She had to be the only woman in Ouachita County who would resist lunch with Drew Griffin.

The Biggest Heart in Choctaw Hollow 47

"It's nice of you to offer, but I really must be going," she said, turning away from him.

He caught her arm. "Come on," he said, steering her to the curb, "everyone has to eat. Besides, you can pick up some of the local color. If you decide not to stick it out in Choctaw Hollow, at least you'll know what you're leaving behind."

She shot him a look of indignation. "Of course I'm going to stick it out."

He responded with a dubious smile as he escorted her across the street. She struggled to keep up with his long strides.

He opened the old-fashioned screen door leading into the café and she was suddenly immersed in a world far different from the bistros and ethnic restaurants to which she'd been accustomed. Country music throbbed softly in the background. The air was thick with friendly banter and the smell of fried foods. On the wall above the row of green plastic-covered booths were scenic pictures which appeared to have been clipped from calendars. The first showed the Ouachitas in a morning fog.

Drew led Brooke to the last empty booth in the café. Along the way he encountered the friendly nods and waves of the townspeople and he stopped to introduce her to a few, including his high school math teacher and his former Little League coach. As they wished her well in Choctaw Hollow, Brooke could see that their feelings for Drew were nothing short of admiration.

"You seem to have no shortage of friends here," she said as they slid into their seats.

"They're more like family, actually," he said. "They've been good to me. In return, I'm trying to be of service to them. It's a very simple matter."

Brooke glanced about the café to examine its rustic, yet shabby charm. Each table was covered with red and white checked oilcloth, the drinks were served in plastic glasses, and a square of tile was missing beneath one of the revolving stools that lined the counter. "Drew, after your time is up in Choctaw Hollow, where will you go?" She genuinely wanted to know, but she also wanted to distract him from the ad a little while longer.

He looked at her with a faintly puzzled expression. "Need I go somewhere?"

"I thought perhaps..." She thought about his years in the city where one could sample exotic foods, visit the latest exhibits, and attend live concerts. "Well, you know what they say about not being able to go home again."

Before he could respond, a middle-aged waitress with tinted red hair, harlequin glasses, and a big smile set two plastic tumblers of ice water before them.

"Don't tell me, Dr. Griffin," she said with pencil poised over her ticket pad. "You want the special and you want your potatoes boiled instead of fried."

"Lizzie, you're wonderful."

"Oh, phooey," she said with a swat of her hand.

Drew introduced her to Brooke, after which the waitress jotted down the same order for her.

She noted that Drew had a special light in his eyes when he talked to the townspeople. For her, his look

The Biggest Heart in Choctaw Hollow 49

was mysterious and mocking, a reminder that he thought she really didn't belong.

Lizzie bent over, and in a low tone said, "I set aside some fresh blackberry cobbler for you this morning." She paused to give Brooke a conspiratorial wink. "Didn't want to run out like last time."

After giving Drew a brief pat on the shoulder, she hustled off toward the kitchen.

Drew followed the woman for a moment with his eyes, then turned to Brooke. "Perhaps that answers your question," he said. "In some respects, it is possible to go home again."

Brooke toyed with her fork. "I think I understand."

He shook his head slowly. "Only a native of these mountains could really understand, but thanks for trying."

"Maybe you should try to understand me sometime," she countered.

He leaned forward slightly. "Let's start with the ad in the newspaper. Why did you circle it?"

Brooke felt the color in her cheeks deepen. "I was exploring the availability of part-time jobs in the area."

"I'm not sure I understand."

"I'm a little short on cash right now because of the accident. I didn't realize at first that it was your ad."

He smiled wryly. "And you changed your mind about applying once you found out."

Brooke smiled ruefully. "Something like that."

He clasped his chin while studying her with faint amusement. "Putting personalities and backgrounds aside for a moment, tell me: What do you know about working in a doctor's office?"

Brooke straightened. "I worked in an inner-city children's clinic after my freshman year of college. The next year, I put together an art program. The year after that, I did the office work in a food bank. I know basic first aid and I know something about office management. Contrary to what you think, I haven't been lounging around all these years asking the maid to peel me some grapes."

Drew arched an eyebrow. "Perhaps, then, you'd make a good hand."

"Not perhaps," she shot back, "would. And add 'certainly' to that."

"When can you start?"

"I'm not starting," she said stubbornly. "I don't want to work for you."

He stared at her quizzically. Before he could respond, Lizzie returned with two steaming plates of meat loaf.

"Enjoy your meal, honey," she said to Drew. "You, too, miss."

Drew picked up his fork but left his food untouched. "Brooke, there aren't many part-time jobs available in Choctaw Hollow. At best, your other options are the Burger Barn or the shirt factory. Can you sew?"

"No," she conceded.

"Well, that takes care of that. As for the Burger Barn, they'd probably prefer a local if there were an opening at all. Somehow, you don't look too—well, needy."

Brooke studied him anxiously, then took a stab at

The Biggest Heart in Choctaw Hollow 51

her meat loaf which she swallowed without tasting. It was clear that she was fortunate to have the one option she had. But of all people to know she was struggling, it had to be him, she thought, giving a piece of potato a jab.

"How about starting tomorrow?" he asked gently. His tone was conciliatory.

She thought of the bills that would be due before her first paycheck, and took a deep breath. "Yes, I can start tomorrow. Thank you."

His expression brightened. "I assume you know that I can't pay much, but the hours are fairly flexible. Saturdays are when I need help the most. The rest of the time, you can come in after school, just a couple of days a week. We can talk about it more tomorrow. Why don't you come in about three-thirty?"

Brooke nodded.

They ate in silence for a few moments. Brooke felt slightly awkward. Their relationship had been a paradoxical one—one of mutual animosity, yet not without its lighter moments. Now there was going to be another factor in this equation—he was going to be her employer. She was going to have to forget her pride and simply do the best job she could. She couldn't allow him to see her stumble again.

"You're not eating much," he observed, studying her half-filled plate. "Don't you like it?"

"It's delicious," she said, "but I'm not used to such big meals at lunch."

"I can see that," he said, his eyes sweeping casually over her body.

Brooke, feeling naked under his blue-gray gaze, reprimanded him with her eyes.

"And now," he said, looking over her shoulder, "it's almost time for the grand finale."

Brooke turned to see Lizzie marching cheerfully up the aisle.

"Ready for cobbler?" she asked, sticking her pencil behind her ear.

"Brooke?" Drew asked.

She shook her head. "No, thank you."

Drew gave Lizzie an uncomprehending shrug. "I'll take some," he said, "a nice, big helping with a sprinkle of sugar on the crust."

Lizzie smiled and hurried toward the kitchen.

"A man has to keep up his strength, you know," Drew said.

Within seconds, the waitress deposited a large bowl of rich purple berries in front of him, then with a quick pat on his shoulder, disappeared.

Drew studied the delicate golden crust, laced with sugar, with apparent relish. "This cobbler is to desserts what the Sistine Chapel is to art," he said, waving his spoon over it. "Now, can you resist?"

She shook her head as the warm, fruity aroma weakened her resolve. She reached for a spoon, but the waitress had already removed her silverware.

"Here," he said, scooping up a spoonful of the pie, "try this."

He carefully aimed the spoon at her mouth. As she opened it, she touched his hand to guide the spoon. Her heart responded with a kick to the warm strength of his fingers. The sensation eclipsed the luscious tartness of the fruit.

"Admit it," he said, his voice rich with confidence. "It's the best you ever had." Without waiting for a response, he scooped out another spoonful and brought it slowly to his own lips. He savored it slowly as his eyes flickered over her face.

"You really shouldn't eat after people, you know," she said, trying to ignore the little spark he'd set off inside her.

"Come to think of it, you're right," he said, his eyes sparkling with mischief. "There was a course on that in medical school. It was called 'Eating After People 101.' Do you suppose I'm in imminent danger of death?"

"Of course not," she mumbled.

"Then have another bite," he said, aiming another spoonful at her. "That way, I won't have to die alone, should it come to that."

Before she could object, the spoon was at her lips and she took another bite. The touch of the spoon to her lips brought an unwanted surge to her pulse. But to Drew, she felt certain, it was simply a playful taste test.

Suddenly quiet, Drew finished the rest of his dessert quickly, then looked at his watch. "It's time to go back to the office," he said. His tone was suddenly crisp and professional, leaving Brooke slightly off guard. There was a light side to this man and it was obvious he had the admiration and respect of many. But there was also the quiet, brooding Drew Griffin that made Brooke wonder if he bore some sort of scar yet tender.

Brooke spent the afternoon at the school in preparation for the classes that she would begin teaching on the following Monday.

Boxes of finger paints and poster board had arrived, along with a supply of charcoal pencils. The cabin roof had been repaired the day before, and for the second day in a row, it hadn't rained. Grandmama apparently was too busy with plans for the upcoming garden show to give her a call. She now had a part-time job that would keep her from going broke before payday. Although there were no luxuries and few diversions and, admittedly, she missed the bustle of life in the city, her life in Choctaw Hollow was beginning to come together.

The battered old truck rattled over every bump as Brooke drove back to the cabin. If Grandmama could see her now, she thought, she'd send Ned after her.

She slipped out of her linen dress and threw on her jeans and, grudgingly, a designer T-shirt Grandmama had bought her. "If you're going to wear those dreadful T-shirts," she'd said, "you should at least wear quality."

For the first time since Brooke had arrived, she set up her easel on the small, covered porch and began to sketch the mountains. The evening sun was poised for a landing on a purple-hued ridge. In the foreground were thickets of trees.

Her feelings of loneliness and uncertainty always faded when she took a pencil or brush in hand. Brooke considered herself a serious and diligent artist, but she painfully remembered the haughty words of one gallery owner: "You haven't lived life, my dear. You don't know what it is to suffer and it shows in your work." Her cheeks stung at the thought of it. She knew a lot about suffering and hence the serene and sometimes playful scenes.

This was Drew's world, she thought, as she shaded in one of the distant ridges. It would only be hers for one year. She thought of the little sparks his touch ignited in her and she felt a twinge of alarm. She was in new surroundings. She was lonely and vulnerable and he was only tolerating her because he needed help.

Her thoughts were interrupted by the crunch of footsteps on gravel. She looked up to find a small boy standing on the edge of the road with a container in his hands. He wore a blue cape over his shorts and T-shirt. Beside him was a large white dog. A patch of black over the animal's eye gave him the look of a pirate.

"Hello," she called with a wave. She recognized him as the child who had peered into her window.

He approached her shyly, the dog at his side, and stepped up on the porch. "Here," he said, handing her a cylinder-shaped parcel. It was wrapped in the Sunday comics, twisted on top and secured with a piece of blue yarn. "I'm supposed to 'pologize for peeping in your window. I'm sorry."

Brooke took the package from him. "That's very sweet of you, Thaney," she said, remembering his unusual name. "Is it all right if I open it now?"

He nodded vigorously, his sable hair gleaming in the evening light.

Brooke removed the wrapping to find a coffee can underneath. Inside were freshly baked chocolate chip cookies. "I bet you didn't know this was my favorite kind, did you?"

He shook his head, studying her with thickly lashed brown eyes.

"They look so delicious that I think I'll have one now," she said, taking one. She offered the can to him. With dirt-smudged fingers, he took two. When he turned to give one to the dog, Brooke noted the Superman emblem on the back of his cape. "Don't tell me you made these yourself," she said.

He grinned shyly, shaking his head. "Granny did." He downed the cookie quickly, then reached for two more, one of which was snapped up by the dog. "My granny knows how to cook wedding cakes, too. Would you like to have one?"

Brooke laughed. "Not just yet."

"She was 'posed to make one for Dr. Drew," he said, licking a smear of chocolate from a finger.

Brooke's heart gave a hard thump. "Is he going to have a wedding?" Her voice was tight.

"No," he said distractedly, eyeing Brooke's sketch. "Wow, you can draw!" He touched the paper, leaving behind a tiny smear of chocolate.

"Would you like me to teach you how?" she asked. Simultaneously, she was trying to comprehend what he'd said about the cake.

"I already know how," he exclaimed proudly.

She passed off the remark as childish bravado, then

returned to the question dogging her mind. "Thaney, why would Dr. Drew need a wedding cake if he wasn't getting married?"

With his finger, the little boy traced the outline of the mountains that Brooke had drawn. "I don't know," he said casually.

The response did little to settle Brooke's anxious curiosity.

"You know what?" he asked, turning suddenly. "Dr. Drew took out my tonsils and noise."

"Adenoids?"

He shook his head. "When I breathed, there was a noise in my nose, and he took it out"

Brooke grinned at her pixielike guest. "He's a good doctor, isn't he?"

"Yep," he said, reaching for another cookie. The can was now half empty. He broke off a piece for the dog. "Bet you can't guess what my dog's name is."

"Whitey?"

"It's Dog," he said with an air of satisfaction. "Well, I'd better go," he said. His short leap over the two porch steps sent his cape aloft.

"Thank you for the cookies," she called after him.

As Dog went bounding after, the porch became strangely quiet. Brooke knew that children had active imaginations, but there was a haunting element of plausibility in the child's story. If there was cake, why wasn't there a wedding? Drew Griffin's personal life shouldn't be her concern, she told herself. Yet it was all she could think about.

* * *

When Brooke arrived at the clinic the next afternoon, the waiting room was half-filled. There was a very expectant mother, a frowning old man tapping the floor nervously with his cane, a woman with a fretful baby, and a sniffling teenager with a stack of fashion magazines. There was no sign of Drew.

Brooke went to an old wooden desk in the corner where an appointment book lay. The desk was layered with unopened mail, file folders, calendars, and a disarray of assorted notes, ledgers, and business cards left by pharmaceutical and equipment salesmen. There was no doubt about it. Drew Griffin was a man in need of office help.

She immediately began organizing, first by putting newly arrived magazines in the magazine rack. But before she could finish, the telephone rang.

"Dr. Griffin's office," she said pleasantly. "An appointment? Certainly. Let's see what's available, she said, flipping through the appointment book. A week into the next month, she found an opening. "Mrs. Benson," she jotted down under 9 a.m. "Arthritis."

Suddenly, the door to the examination room clicked open, and Drew appeared. His eyes met hers for a short, but intense moment that made her blood stir.

Wearing jeans, a denim shirt, and a crisp white lab coat, he strolled toward her. "I'm much busier today than I anticipated. I'm not sure how much longer it will be before we can discuss the office."

"Don't worry," Brooke said brightly. "Instead of talking, I'll do something. I'll put the reception desk in order and answer the phone."

"If you'd just answer the phone, I'd be grateful,"

The Biggest Heart in Choctaw Hollow

he said. "Usually, one of the patients ends up answering it. He turned to the appointment book. Who's first?

"Mr. Feeney," Brooke said.

Drew turned to the old man. "Good afternoon, Mr. Feeney," he said, touching his shoulder. "Let's see about that knee."

One by one, the patients went in and out while Brooke tried to turn disorder into order. She'd scheduled three more appointments and now it was possible to see the varnished oak top of what appeared to be a teacher's desk.

Finally, close to six o'clock, everyone had left. Drew, his face etched with fatigue, came from the examination room and sat on one of the waiting room benches. He placed his arms along the back of the bench and stretched out his long legs. An errant lock of hair fell across his forehead.

"How was your first day?" he asked, his tone professional.

"Hectic," she said.

He grinned wryly. "Get used to it. This is fairly typical. Since his wife died, Mr. Feeney has been coming in once a month, I think more for companionship than his knee. Katie Harmon could go into labor any day now and little Freddie Watson's immunizations needed updating. The teenager, Callie McGee, is bothered by allergies. It looks like I'm going to have to send her to a specialist. As you'll see, many of the cases I see are fairly routine—stitching cuts, prenatal care, monitoring chronic illnesses such as diabetes. But it's very satisfying work. You get to know people well and they're very appreciative of the extra attention they get in a rural practice."

Brooke could hear the devotion in his voice. There was a bond between him and the people of Choctaw Hollow. Were they his entire life? What of the women there must surely have been?

He ran a hand over his well-formed jaw. "Come on," he said, rising, "let me show you a few things."

She followed him to the examination room, where he showed her where the most commonly used drugs and supplies were.

"It's important to know these things," he said, "because sometimes I will need your help."

"But I'm not a nurse," she protested gently.

"I know, but there are simple fetch-and-carry chores you can do that help me save time, and in medicine, sometimes time can be of the essence. Mrs. Jackson, who preceded you, performed some of these duties as well. It's part of the job."

"I understand," she said.

"You'll learn as we go," he said. "I'd like to stress that reliability is one of the keys to this job. I need someone I can always depend on to do the job right."

"You can depend on me," Brooke assured him. "If you're unsatisfied with me in any way, I'll step aside so you can get someone else."

"I'm glad that's understood," he said.

They talked about bookkeeping and schedules and other details of the job. Brooke agreed to come in on Thursday and Friday afternoons, and on Saturdays. Just as she was preparing to leave, Drew's pager sounded.

The Biggest Heart in Choctaw Hollow   61

"Emergency," he said, quickly grabbing the telephone receiver and punching in a set of numbers. At first, he listened carefully. "Keep pressure on the wound and bring him in," he said.

He turned to Brooke. "A chain saw accident," he said. "A timber company employee."

Brooke instinctively followed him into the examination room and stood helplessly by while he layered the examination table with a special covering and placed needed equipment and supplies on a tray. He asked Brooke to open a set of double doors leading to a driveway in the back. As soon as she did, she could hear the wail of an ambulance siren. Within moments, it was deafeningly close, and the vehicle appeared.

Drew stood by as two paramedics brought in a man on a gurney. His jeans had been cut away from one leg and a thick pad placed over the wound was already soaked with blood. The patient's face was ashen.

Drew quickly donned surgical gloves as the groaning man was transferred to the examination table. He carefully removed the bandage to expose a massive, gaping cut on the man's thigh.

As he gently reassured the patient and quickly went about tending the wound, Brooke's skin turned clammy and beads of sweat popped out all over her skin. The light in the room seemed to dim. She fought the queasiness by taking deep breaths, but it was too late. She felt her body sway.

From the depths of what seemed to be a dream, she heard Drew order: "Hurry, bring me that tray with the supplies on it."

She struggled to comply, but instead collapsed in a heap on the floor.

Chapter Five

The next thing she knew, there was something cold and wet on her forehead. The room came into slow focus and Brooke discovered it was she who was on the examination table. Then the realization of what had happened descended on her like a crushing force. Her insides crumpled. "Oh, no," she muttered.

"Take it easy," Drew said, quickly appearing at her side.

"The man... How is he?" She tried to get up, but he nudged her back down.

"I got him stabilized and they took him on to the hospital. It's forty miles away. He's going to need surgery."

Ignoring his orders, she sat up unsteadily, holding the wet compress in place with one hand. He placed a bracing hand on her shoulder. The warmth and strength of his touch sent a little flutter through her.

The Biggest Heart in Choctaw Hollow   63

"I've let you down and I'm very sorry," she said. "An office assistant who passes out at the sight of blood is not a great asset to a doctor."

The corner of his mouth twitched downward. "I can't say that she is."

Her eyes met his in a moment of sick realization. If she'd been hired on probation, she most certainly failed it.

"I thought you'd worked in a clinic before," he said. She was grateful that there was no hint of anger in his voice.

"It was a pediatric clinic," she said. "It was shots and chicken pox and things like that. I never saw a serious injury like today."

He looked uncomfortable. "You're going to have to do better than this. I can't end up with two patients every time one comes in bleeding."

Her cheeks tingled. It was clear that the job she needed was hanging by a thread. Now, without any doubt, he saw her as naive and sheltered, as being too soft for the challenges ordinary people face every day. She could see it in his cool, blue-gray eyes. But she was determined not to be seen that way, especially by Drew Griffin.

"Please give me another chance," she said. "If there is just one more problem, you can find someone else."

Drew stroked his chin thoughtfully. "I'll agree to that," he said finally.

"Thank you," she said with a sigh of relief. "You won't have to worry about me again. You'll see." But the ghost of doubt lurked in the background. Could it be guaranteed that it would never happen again?

Her first day of school helped her forget her blunders as an office assistant. On Monday, she started with the primary grades. The first graders finger painted, most for the first time. She had the second graders draw crayon pictures of their homes and their families. Third graders drew pictures of themselves doing their favorite activities.

It was among the second graders that she found Thaney. The impish little Choctaw tackled his project eagerly, producing a picture of himself and his grandmother in front of their little yellow house. Brooke was instantly struck by the detail and accuracy of the rendering. It was the work of a child years older.

"It's very, very good, Thaney," she said, looking over his small shoulder as he worked.

"See?" he said, holding up the piece proudly. "I told you I already knew how to draw."

"Who taught you?"

"Nobody," he said simply.

The children drew houses and families of all kinds. She was surprised to see that many of the homes were actually trailers. She noted with concern that some of the children were pale, thin, and shabbily dressed.

Mr. Krauthammer nodded solemnly when she told him later of some of her observations.

"On occasion, there have been people living in the mountains in lean-tos and tents," he explained, "children included. In fact, there have been cases of some

The Biggest Heart in Choctaw Hollow 65

people not sending their kids to school because they didn't have the proper clothing.''

Brooke stared at him in disbelief. "Aren't there agencies to help?"

"Not many, but some folks are too proud to accept help anyway. What they really want is steady work, not charity. Employment in the timber industry goes up and down like a yo-yo, but it's better than nothing and it's all some of them know."

He walked with her to the doorway of the school. It had begun to rain again. The drops pummeled the ground like thousands of little wet fists. "Here it comes again," he said, shaking his head. "I can't ever remember a year like this. More rain means more temporary layoffs."

Brooke put on the wide-brimmed yellow rain hat that matched her slicker and said good-bye to the principal.

"Hope your roof holds this time," he said with a chuckle.

But the little joke didn't do much to distract her from her thoughts about the children. It was a hard life that some of them and their parents led, she mused.

She hurried to the truck and jumped inside. She had learned to maneuver it without too much difficulty. It was awkward, but she liked to think of it as a symbol of her growing adaptability and independence.

She sat in the pickup for a moment watching the last of the faculty depart, leaving her alone in the parking lot. She was going to like her work here, she thought. These children needed the release of art in their lives.

She was due at the clinic soon, but a glance at her watch told her she had ample time. She turned the key in the ignition, but there was no response except a dull grind. Tensing, she leaned forward and tried it again. The noise repeated itself again. She jiggled the key in desperation, but all she got was a sputter and a growl. She glanced at her watch and swallowed hard. She had fifteen minutes left to get to the clinic. She sucked in a sharp breath and gave the steering wheel a punch of frustration. At that instant, the rain fell out of the sky as if she'd knocked it loose. There was nothing to do but start walking.

It was only six blocks to the clinic, but Brooke was soaked by the time she got to the end of the first. Her feet squished in her shoes, marking a sloshy rhythm to her frustration. When would things stop going wrong? Was Choctaw Hollow jinxed?

A strong gust of wind blew rain under her collar and down the back of her neck. She could feel it trickle down her back. Her finely tailored khaki pants were soaked, her Italian loafers possibly ruined. It wasn't the clothes that mattered, it was getting to the clinic on time. She'd started out with time to spare and now the clock was swiftly working against her. She broke into a run. Considering her record so far, she couldn't afford to be late.

She made it to the clinic with two minutes to spare, leaving a puddle inside the entryway. She took off her slicker and hat, but she was soaked from the knees down. Her hair was damp, droplets of water ran down

The Biggest Heart in Choctaw Hollow 67

her face, and her shoes oozed with water. Half of the front of her shirt was wet.

There were four patients in the waiting room and when she looked up, they were all watching and wearing wry little smiles of understanding.

"Haven't seen the likes of this weather since fifty-two," a bent old man said. "It was so wet that year that all the fish drowned."

His chuckle was joined by the others in the group. Brooke, now shivering, smiled despite her discomfort.

Suddenly, the door to the examination room opened and a woman with a fresh bandage on her thumb emerged. Close behind was Drew. His gaze flicked over Brooke's drenched form and his eyes widened.

She winced apologetically. "Could I possibly borrow a towel?"

"You're going to need more than a towel," he said. "Go into my apartment and get out of those clothes. Get a scrub suit off the top shelf of my closet. There are also clean socks in a laundry basket. It's not haute couture, but it will do."

Brooke nodded, not unmindful of another little skeptical reference to her background. She wanted him to take her seriously. Yet every time she tried to demonstrate her capability, she failed.

She left her soaked shoes at the door and quickly went inside his quarters. Uneasily, she stepped into his bedroom. It was a small room containing an old iron bedstead painted black and a vintage oak chest. Brooke was surprised to see that the bed was made, although inexpertly. A handmade quilt with fan designs lay unevenly over the bed. A braided rug which appeared to be made from old plaid flannel shirts was almost obscured by a scattering of books and medical journals on the floor. A striped valence hung over the single window. It was clear that Drew had been amply mothered by some of the women of Choctaw Hollow.

Brooke took one of a half dozen scrub suits from the closet shelf and found a pair of thick cotton socks on top the heap of laundry in a large wicker basket. She took off her partially wet garments, hanging them over the shower curtain in the bathroom. As she toweled herself dry, she became aware of Drew's spicy scent in the room and felt an unwelcome twitter in her veins. She was being silly, she told herself scoldingly, to show any reaction to a man who didn't like her. And despite his attractiveness and obvious devotion to his patients, what was there to like about him? she asked herself.

She dressed quickly, but the top of the green scrubs hung halfway to her knees, the V neck much too low. To hitch it up, she managed a small knot on the back of the neck. The pants came with a drawstring which she struggled to tighten sufficiently. She cuffed the legs up several times over. She pulled the socks up as high as she could to avoid tripping on the toes. Self-consciously, she went back to her desk. She returned the looks of the bemused patients with an embarrassed smile.

She was seated at her desk opening the day's mail when Drew emerged from the room carrying a baby. Brooke noted the ease with which he carried the child in the crook of his arm. It was as if he were born knowing how.

"Brooke, I need to see little Andy again in a

month," he said. At that moment, the baby grabbed a fistful of his hair and gave a hard yank. Drew's eyes widened in surprise and then he broke into laughter. It was a full, rich, from-the-heart laugh that Brooke had never heard before from this man whose seriousness sometimes gravitated toward melancholy. It exposed a side of him that she'd never seen before.

He loosened the baby's grip, muttered something about a "Samson in the making," then gave him a playful bounce before handing him back to his mother. She was a chubby, smiling woman who wore a sweatshirt with a picture of a cocker spaniel on the front.

After getting a nod from the mother, Brooke jotted down the baby's name and appointment date on a card and handed it to her.

"Occupational hazard," Drew said after they left. He gave the affected spot on his scalp a quick rub. "Who's next?"

Brooke stepped from behind the desk and called Mrs. Collins. A heavy woman with ruddy cheeks rose to her feet. She directed her toward the examination room. After she ushered the woman inside, she turned to find Drew studying her. There was a hint of amusement on his lips, but he said nothing.

Eyeing him back, Brooke testily gave her pants a quick hitch and sat back down.

As Drew tended to his patient, she called Frank Harjo, who promised to tend to the pickup immediately. If he couldn't, she explained, she had no transportation tomorrow to her classes in a neighboring town. She hung up with a deep sigh. It might be another week before her car was ready, he'd said. What else could go wrong? she thought. Yet she didn't want to contemplate it any further.

Drew's business affairs were in worse shape than she'd thought. In the three weeks since Mrs. Jackson had gone, nothing had been entered in the books. There were dozens of pages of medical notes that needed to be transcribed and statements to be typed. Brooke noted the odd absence of a computer in the office. As she was making mental notes of how to get things back in order, the telephone rang.

"It's Jenny Hadley." There was an anxious tenor to the caller's voice. "My son has cut his finger badly on a piece of glass," she said. "Would you ask Drew if he can see him immediately?"

Brooke punched in the number of the phone in the next room and briefed him on the call.

"Tell her I'll be waiting," he said.

Brooke hung up, swallowing hard at the prospect of another bloody injury. She took several deep breaths before tackling the paperwork again.

Drew was finished with Mrs. Collins by the time Jenny Hadley burst through the front door. She carried a screaming boy who appeared to be about four. His face was red and streaked with tears. Blood stained the front of his T-shirt, and his other hand, clutched protectively against his small chest, was wrapped in a small purple towel. Brooke winced, closed her eyes, and took another deep breath.

Drew and the mother exchanged quick greetings. Drew knelt and faced the crying boy. "It's all right," he said. "Come with me. We'll make it well."

The boy's sobs softened to sniffles until Drew

The Biggest Heart in Choctaw Hollow 71

placed him on the examination table. Once he eyed the instruments and the unfamiliar surroundings, he let out a series of fresh, choking wails.

While he howled, Brooke apologized to the two waiting patients. But before she could get back to her desk, Drew appeared at the door. "I may need your help. Would you come in here please?"

When she stepped into the room, it was clear that neither doctor nor mother was having much success in calming the boy. The mother, an attractive blond who appeared to be in her early thirties, was now in tears herself. As she held him, Drew unwrapped the towel from his hand to reveal a jagged inch-long cut in the side of his index finger.

Her stomach churning at the sight of it, Brooke took in a gulp of air to steady herself.

"He's going to need about three stitches, Jenny," Drew said.

The woman nodded.

Drew gave Brooke a look of concern. "Get me the suture kit while I prepare some injections."

Brooke complied, then watched Drew try to calm the boy again. In a gentle tone, he asked if he'd seen various children's movies and inquired about toys and pets. The boy quit crying long enough to answer his questions, but when Drew gently explained that he was going to have to give him a shot in the finger so the stitches wouldn't hurt, the boy let out a scream of resistance.

Brooke, whose head was beginning to ache, felt a pang of sympathy for Drew. Instinctively, she quickly ran to her desk for a black marker and several sheets of paper.

She held a sheet up in front of the boy. "I can draw your picture," she said. "Would you like to see?"

The child blinked at her through his tears.

"Look," she said, studying his round facial features and tousled hair. She quickly sketched a fretful boy as his crying dwindled to a series of sniffles.

"Now, I'll show you what you'll look like when Dr. Griffin makes you well." She drew more slowly this time, adding details and a broad smile. She added a beret and a uniform. "This picture is for you to take home and show your friends. But first, you must try to be a brave soldier."

The boy nodded tearfully.

"And while the doctor fixes your finger, I'll draw some pictures of him and you can watch. Would you like that?"

He nodded again, wiping a tear away.

Brooke stood beside the child and began to sketch. The child was sufficiently absorbed that Drew was able to inject the anesthetic in his finger with only a minimum of resistance. Adding her praise to the mother's, she went back to the earlier sketch she'd done of the boy and drew a medal on the uniform. It was a star suspended on a ribbon. In doing it, Brooke managed to tweak a faint smile from the child's lips.

After a few moments, Drew began making the stitches. The boy's whimpering stopped as she sketched the doctor patiently working.

"Put Mommy in, too," he said, uttering his first sentence since he'd arrived.

The Biggest Heart in Choctaw Hollow 73

"Indeed, I will," she said as she added more details.

Drew's bottom lip protruded slightly as he concentrated on his work and Brooke's heart gave a little twinge.

As she began to sketch the mother, who had winced through the whole ordeal, she realized that her drawing had not only calmed the boy but herself. Her own queasiness over the sight of blood had almost been forgotten.

"All done," Drew proclaimed after wrapping a bandage around the finger. He tousled the boy's sandy hair. "You were very good."

Brooke added another medal to one of the sketches. "That one is for being an extra brave soldier." She handed the drawings to him and the boy responded with a look of awe.

As Drew lifted the child off the table, he gave Brooke a smile of gratitude. Her heart fluttered, making her glad that he wasn't terribly generous with them. His smiles were entirely too arresting. They could make a woman lose her senses.

As the boy hurried out of the room, his mother thanked both of them. Then she turned to the doctor. "How have you been, Drew?" she asked with the tone of a longtime friend.

"Fine."

"Time is getting away, isn't it? Do you realize that it was fourteen years ago this spring that we graduated from high school?"

"When you're as busy as I am, you don't have time to realize much of anything," he said lightly.

"Maybe that's good," she said. "My birthday last week was also a reminder of the passing years." There was a brief pause. "I . . . I got a card from Cheryl."

Drew's eyes darkened. "How is she?" Brooke detected a tightness in his voice.

"She's quite a businesswoman. The real estate firm that she started has expanded to three locations. That's pretty much her life. She went after the big city, the bright lights and success, and now has them all. She has everything but a husband, not that she's lacking for prospects."

Drew unbuttoned his collar and loosened his tie. "I wish her well. Please give her my regards," he said stiffly.

The woman nodded. Her smile seemed a bit awkward. "I will," she said, giving Drew's arm a squeeze. "Take care of yourself."

"I think I can do that," he said with a terse smile.

As he walked Jenny Hadley and her son to the door, explaining how to care for the wound, Brooke pondered their exchange. Cheryl was obviously someone who had meant something to Drew. Perhaps, she thought with a twinge of regret, a spark was still there.

She went back to her work while he saw the two remaining patients. In the interim, much to her relief, Frank Harjo called to say that the truck was now in running order. There was something about water and a distributor cap that Brooke didn't quite understand, but it didn't matter anyway as long as it was fixed.

When the last patient left, Drew appeared at her desk.

"Brooke, you were terrific with that kid." There

was a glint of approval in his eyes. "Your help was invaluable."

A slow smile spread across her face. "Thank you. I'm glad I was of more use today than yesterday."

A faint smile played across his lips. "I would have to say that you were."

"Why doesn't all that blood bother you?"

"You get used to it. Pretend it's ketchup."

Brooke laughed softly.

She caught him studying her for a fleeting moment and it made her blood surge.

"On Sunday, why don't you let me show you the area?" he asked. "I'll admit there's not much to see but the mountains, but there are some very nice spots. I'll get Gertie from the Green Tomato to box up a picnic supper for us." Then, as if he were uncertain as to how she might interpret his invitation, he added, "If you're going to work here, you should get a better understanding of the area."

"Of course," she said with equal caution. "That's important. It would be very nice of you to show me."

"Gladly," he said, his tone businesslike. "Shall I pick you up around one?"

"That would be fine," she said, standing.

His eyes followed her movements. "By the way, keep the scrubs. You may need them again. I'd suggest taking a tuck here and there though. They could slide right off you." His gaze swept over her as if he might be relishing the thought.

She shot him a sour look. "Perhaps you could quit making jokes long enough to recommend a tailor."

His expression bordered on playful. "There are no

tailors in Choctaw Hollow. See Jessie Johnico. She can fix them for you."

"In the meantime, I'll change," she said, giving him a look of impatience.

She walked briskly into his apartment and put on her clothes, although they were still soaked. She came out with the scrubs folded and tucked under her arm. Drew, sitting on the edge of her desk, stood. But the mirthful look he'd had moments before was replaced with one that looked slightly troubled.

"Anything wrong?" she asked.

He shook his head distractedly and wished her a good night.

Baffled over his change of mood, Brooke, not wanting to ask for help, hiked the five blocks to Frank Harjo's garage.

Sunday turned out to be a warm, clear October day illuminated with rays of ocher sunshine. She was on the porch working on the final stages of her mountain watercolor when she sighted the Jeep as it turned off the highway. She tried to ignore the quickening of her pulse.

She wasn't sure how to take Drew even though she knew how he took her—as someone playing at real life, who could run back to the shelter of privilege and affluence whenever she was ready. He was alternately friendly and aloof, keeping her perpetually off balance. It was as if he had guards posted around himself. She sensed he'd been hurt deeply before. If so, that made two of them.

The Jeep came to a stop behind the pickup and Drew sauntered toward her. He was clad in khakis and

The Biggest Heart in Choctaw Hollow 77

a pale blue oxford shirt rolled up at the sleeves. His expression was serious, but there was a glint of mirth in his eyes. "For someone not living in the style to which she is accustomed, you look quite comfortable," he said.

Brooke stood back from her easel, her brush still in her hand. "I'm always happy when I'm painting."

He stepped to her side, examining her work. He was so close, she could feel the heat from his body. Feeling a faint stirring in her blood, she stepped away from him and toward the easel. "It's very good. You've not only captured the colors, but the mood. This is not just something you play at, is it?" he said, an eyebrow slightly elevated in surprise.

"Grandmama thinks it is," she responded. "She thinks real artists live in garrets and starve. Who would want that sort of life?"

"I see," he said, perusing the picture from another angle. "She thinks you should have more practical pursuits?"

"Yes, like becoming a figure of high society and marrying some money to add to our own."

He smiled wryly. "You've had a rough life. I can tell."

She set her jaw and gave him a resentful glance. "It has been more complicated than you think."

"Come on," he said, ignoring the remark. "I promised you a tour."

They began in the southern portion of the county, with the timber industry that supported many of the people of Choctaw Hollow. From the highway, Brooke could see acres of seedlings, saplings, and rough-cut logs, and dozens of small logging roads leading into the woods. But it was Drew of whom she was most conscious. At the very moment her mind was inventing ways to put him in his place once and for all, her heart was stirring at the nearness of him. In such close quarters, his solid shoulders, darkly lashed pale eyes, and spicy scent couldn't be ignored.

"You're behaving yourself quite nicely," he said, casting a sardonic glance at her. "What are you thinking?"

"You don't want to know," she said. She'd just created a mental image of his getting mired in the mud and having to suffer the indignity of being rescued by her, a "pampered" heiress whom he surely thought was unaccustomed to lifting anything heavier than a teacup.

"It must be interesting then," he said with a hint of a smile.

She glanced at him quickly, her mouth quirked in mild irritation. Couldn't he take anything that she said seriously?

"Well, if you won't tell me what you're thinking," he said, "I'll tell you what I'm thinking."

Brooke responded with silence.

"My family goes back four generations in these mountains," he said. "My great-grandfather came to help build the railroad through here. Then the timber industry began to grow and that was my grandfather's livelihood, my father's as well.

"My father died when I was eleven. My mother supported my brother and me by working in the shirt factory. Now, there's just me.'' His voice had an undercurrent of sadness.

"I'll spare you the story of my great-grandfather, William Crosswaite," Brooke said almost guiltily. "You've probably heard it."

"He was the barber who struck oil," Drew said, pulling the Jeep to the shoulder. He did a turnabout, then headed in the opposite direction. "Now, let's go see the best the mountains have to offer."

The highway became a curling ribbon, winding up hills lush with trees. Brooke's artist's eye took in the tones of blue and green that lightened in the distance. The hills were rimmed with a golden light. Wispy white clouds drifted across the sky. The hills and valleys were much higher and steeper than the ones Brooke had seen when she first arrived at Choctaw Hollow.

"Beautiful," she said. "I didn't know such sights existed here."

Drew pulled over to an observation turnout and stopped the car. "See, not all the excitement is in the city."

Awed, Brooke jumped out of the Jeep and stood near the railing, letting the wind twist through her hair. The air smelled of pine and cedar. In town, it had been warm, but at the higher elevation, the breeze left chill bumps on her bare arms.

Drew walked over and stood so close behind her that she could feel the heat of his body. Her pulse quickened.

"My father taught me a lot about the flora and fauna of these mountains," he said. "We used to play a game in which I would have to identify trees and plants by their leaves."

Brooke turned toward him, noting a nostalgic look in his eyes. She sensed that his heart would always be here.

"Grandmama taught me how to identify people, as in people on the social register," she said. "When I was four, I caused a sensation when I told Mr. Blassengame, the banker, that his hair was on crooked. At first, I didn't understand what I'd done wrong. After all, I'd identified him correctly."

A deep, gentle laugh rolled from Drew's throat. "Shame on you."

He turned, opened up the back of the Jeep, and pulled out a cooler. "This is the perfect backdrop for a picnic. How's your appetite?"

"I'm starved."

Gertie had packed fried chicken, potato salad, cole slaw, baked beans, and two huge servings of peach cobbler, which they spread out on a checkered cloth on the tailgate.

"When I first arrived back in Choctaw Hollow, it seemed like every other woman in town was bringing me something to eat," he said. "At one point, I had seven cakes in the house. I ended up taking them to the Little League, which polished them off in a hurry."

Brooke, still chilled by the mountain air, ate with relish. The food reminded her of Hannah's Labor Day picnics and she suddenly felt a twinge of homesickness. The mountains were beautiful, but so were Grandmama's glorious chrysanthemums.

The Biggest Heart in Choctaw Hollow

"You're thinking again," Drew said.

"You're being nosy again," she returned. "Furthermore, you have a smear of mayonnaise on your cheek."

He wiped his cheek with his index finger.

"You missed. Higher," she directed.

He missed again.

She reached out and touched his cheek. It was hot and mildly abrasive, and made her pulse leap.

"Thanks," he said, unaffectedly.

For the first time in her life, Brooke felt almost shy as she finished her meal. If there were any sparks in the air here, they were coming solely from her.

Suddenly, the light, which had been so golden and pure, turned to pewter and there was a faint, yet ominous rumble in the distance. "Oh, no," Brooke wailed, "not rain again."

Even Drew, who had seemed so far to take the rain in stride, looked disappointed as he finished his peach cobbler.

They put everything away and he quickly snapped the tailgate shut just as they were hit by a gust of wind carrying little droplets of rain. A dissonant squawking came from overhead.

"Look, Drew," she said, stepping away from the car, "geese."

He stood beside her. "The old-timers would say that's a sign. Winter's coming early this year."

"Look what the light has done to the mountains now," she said. The deep greens and blues had gone to indigo and purple. "I wish I could paint it right now."

As she studied the scene, another damp gust brought a new crop of chill bumps to her arms. Shivering, she rubbed them briskly.

Suddenly, Drew embraced her from behind to shelter her from the chill and she melted willingly against him, her heart kicking. Then he turned her slowly toward him and lowered his lips to hers.

Chapter Six

The kiss was at first tentative. It began with a soft touch of his lips against hers, then took on an increasing fervor. In its heat, Brooke sensed a deep yearning.

She couldn't have turned away from him if she'd wanted to. It was as if some force, as strong as the gravity holding the mountains in place, had locked them together. The tenderness of his embrace, the warmth of his touch, were too much to resist.

His touch left her dizzy and for an instant made her forget everything—the drizzle, the wind, and the isolation of Choctaw Hollow. His body was hard and strong. The shelter of arms was like a long-sought haven. Then, as the world began to flood back into her consciousness, she was reminded that such feelings in the past had led to pain.

Drew's lips suddenly left hers and he released her.

Still dazed, she looked up into his eyes. They were murky with emotion.

"It's time to go back." His voice was tight.

She nodded, her mind too muddled for words. He helped her inside the car, and as they drove away, the silence between them was overpowering. The sheer surprise of the kiss had left her off-balance, but her reaction to it was even more unexpected.

As if to fill the void, he inserted a tape in the dash and soft, classical music began to play. She stole a glance at him to find his expression slightly troubled. His lower lip protruded slightly and his eyes were narrowed in concentration.

"Drew, it's all right," she said, breaking the silence.

He took a deep breath. "It was unplanned, Brooke. It just happened. I don't make a habit of kissing my office assistants, so I apologize. Consider it a lapse, if you will."

"You didn't enjoy it?" she asked.

His eyes snapped to her, then his expression softened. "But I did," he said huskily.

"Then why are you sorry?" she asked boldly.

"Because life is complicated, Brooke," he said, slowing to take a curve.

She felt an inexplicable pang of disappointment. It was clear that he considered her one of its complications.

Drew was right, she later conceded. They were two people from two different worlds. She would be leav-

The Biggest Heart in Choctaw Hollow 85

ing; he would be staying. Kisses like that would only complicate matters.

For the next few evenings, she sketched and painted and carefully planned lessons. It helped stave off the loneliness that hung in the quiet of the night. Since Drew's quiet good-bye days ago, the silence at the cabin had been piercing.

She'd conducted classes now in all four schools in her circuit and found the children thirsty for creative expression. She found the proportion of poverty in the outlying areas was even higher.

Brooke had become self-conscious of her fine gabardine blazers and meticulously tailored skirts. They had attracted curious looks from students and teachers alike. She had recently begun wearing jeans and laced boots that she'd ordered by mail. She often paired the jeans with white shirts and silk scarves. Perhaps she'd never be mistaken for a local, but at least she felt less conspicuous.

She was sketching the living room of the cabin, trying to keep her thoughts away from Drew, when the telephone rang.

"How are you, my dear?" The perfectly modulated voice was unmistakable.

"Hello, Grandmama." On this long night, Brooke was genuinely happy to hear her grandmother's voice. "Yes, I'm fine."

"Well, I can't say as much for myself," said Grandmama dropping the familiar cue to inquire about her health.

"Poor dear." Brooke settled on the sofa in preparation for a long story. "What's wrong?"

"It's my heart again. Irregular little beats when I least expect them. It's worry, Brooke. I read in the paper about all that rain down in the mountains and how parts of the highway have simply slid away. Do come home, dear, and stop this nonsense before you come to harm. You're a city girl. You're not used to those kinds of conditions."

"But I'm happy here," she said, giving the truth a bit of a stretch.

"You've forgotten all about your poor Grandmama," she said with a clearly audible sniff. "I have no one left in this family but you, you must remember."

"I remember."

"I thought surely you'd be home by now." Her tone was wistful. "Home to stay."

"No, Grandmama," she said firmly.

She heard a raspy breath on the other end of the line. "At least come home for Thanksgiving, just for a few days."

"Christmas," she corrected. "There's so much to do here and not enough time to rush home for Thanksgiving."

"But how could you not?" The old lady's disappointment was audible.

"We'll make up for it at Christmas," she said. "Besides, aren't they having a Thanksgiving dinner at the country club?"

"Yes, dear, but it's hardly the same."

Brooke thought she heard a sniff. "I'm sorry, but it's best if I stay here."

Brooke hung up filled with guilt. Oddly, thoughts

The Biggest Heart in Choctaw Hollow 87

of going home filled her with an unexpected flicker of yearning and Christmas seemed an eternity away. It wasn't the mountains or the loneliness that she wanted to escape. It was a disturbing rumbling in her heart.

The end of the week brought more rain and along with it a hint of winter. The wind howled, the rain blew, and the mercury dropped. It was then that she realized the cabin had no heat except for the fireplace. And for that, there wasn't a single piece of wood. To add to that, there weren't enough blankets.

On Friday morning, she sat swaddled in a heavy terry cloth robe at the kitchen table. It was then that she began to sniffle and feel a vague hint of a cold in the making. Her fingernails had turned a dusty shade of blue. At school, it would be warm, she thought with delicious anticipation. She would feel much better.

She didn't. By the time she arrived at the clinic, her head felt like a bubble on the verge of bursting.

To make matters worse, the waiting room was filled to capacity. Children fretted on their mothers' laps, adults leafed impatiently through magazines or simply stared at the wall. An elderly woman worked on a doily, her crochet needle quickly darting to and fro.

Brooke had settled at her desk and begun catching up on her paperwork when she heard a door open. A woman with a small child in her arms exited. Drew followed, his tie loosened, his white coat rolled up at the elbows. At the sight of him, Brooke's heart gave a little kick. He glanced up and for an instant, their gazes locked. The moment seemed to bring a mutual reminder that things between them would never be the same.

"Hello, Brooke," he said, his tone businesslike. He laid the records of the previous patient on her desk. "Would you call the next patient, please?" His tall form disappeared behind the door again, as she sent a mother and child in to see him.

His silence and distance all week had already indicated to Brooke that he'd wanted to reinstate that distance between them. Perhaps he could do that, Brooke thought. Doctors were trained to be dispassionate, to develop shields around their hearts. But she wasn't nearly so skilled at that, despite the emotional bumps and bruises she'd suffered.

It was after seven by the time the last patient left. By then, Brooke was sneezing like the Seven Dwarfs cartoon character. With each sneeze, it seemed as though her head were expanding and contracting. Her forehead, to her dismay, was uncomfortably warm.

Drew, his eyes underscored with fatigue, strode out of the examination room, stopping abruptly at her desk. "Let me take a look at you."

Brooke shook her head. "I'll save you the trouble. I have a cold."

Ignoring her, he disappeared into the next room, then came out again, popping a thermometer into her mouth. Shaking her head, she made grunting noises of protest.

After a moment, he plucked it out. "You have a slight fever."

He examined her throat. "Go home and get some rest before it turns into something worse than a cold."

The Biggest Heart in Choctaw Hollow 89

His tone was professional. "You're not accustomed to the strain of two jobs."

Brooke gave him a piercing look. "I wish you wouldn't insist on thinking of me as a member of the leisure class."

He raised an eyebrow. "Then how would you describe yourself?"

"I'm a hard worker, am I not?" Her tone was heated.

A spark of amusement appeared in his eyes. "I can't say that you aren't. But the question is: Have you always been? Who polished the silver, cleaned the oven, and took out the garbage at your house?"

"That was then. This is now," she shot back, daubing at her nose.

"That's precisely what I mean," he said with a flicker of a smile. "You're not used to pushing yourself so hard. That can affect a person's resistance. Tomorrow, I want you to stay home, drink plenty of liquids, and get some rest."

Her spine straightened. "But I can't. There's a ton of work to be done and you've got thirteen patients coming in tomorrow."

"I'll manage." His mouth had a determined crook to one corner. "Stay home. You don't need to be sharing your cold with the patients." His tone softened. "It usually works the other way around."

She gave a deep sigh of resignation.

"And stay warm." His eyes were intense.

She bit her bottom lip. "Could you loan me a blanket?" she asked tentatively. "The cabin has no heat."

His eyes widened. "None?"

"The fireplace is the only heat source." There was a growing stuffiness in her voice. "The cool weather caught me off-guard. I didn't think to get firewood."

"I see." He turned away, took a few paces and stroked his jaw contemplatively. Then he turned back toward her. "Stay here. I'll take the truck and get a few ricks of wood. Then we'll go to the cabin and I'll help you get a fire going."

"Drew, really," she protested. "An extra blanket will do until tomorrow."

He scolded her with his eyes. "I won't be long." He took off his lab coat, hung it on a peg beside her desk, and strode out the door.

His exit was punctuated with a sneeze. She blew her nose, then gave a sigh of exasperation. Why was it that he always managed to see her looking less than hearty and not quite up to the challenges of mountain living? In a pique, she bit the inside of her cheek.

Despite the throbbing of her head, she busied herself getting everything in order for Saturday. Patient records were taken out and placed in a portable file in the order that they would be seen. She typed up a few more bills and was addressing an envelope when Drew returned.

"You're pushing yourself again."

She turned to find him frowning at her. His hair was covered with mist. "You're set up for tomorrow," she said, pretending she didn't note his disapproval.

"Come on," he said. "I'll follow you to the cabin."

It was almost dark by the time they arrived, and the air was heavy with mist and a piercing chill. Brooke,

The Biggest Heart in Choctaw Hollow 91

standing in the living room with a box of tissues in one hand, watched as Drew carried in an armful of split logs as if they were almost weightless. He placed them on the grate and within moments, there was a golden blaze in the hearth.

He got up and turned toward her. The firelight brought out the sparkle in his eyes. "I'm going to make you something hot to drink. What would you like?"

"It's all right, Drew. I can get it. You should go home and get some rest yourself." But what she'd said and what she'd felt were two different things. She wanted him with her. Despite his apparent misgivings toward her, despite their differences, despite the uncertainty and impracticality of their relationship, he had an unwanted effect on her.

He placed his hands on his hips. "You're a terrible patient."

"Thanks for the subtle hint," she said, her eyes fixed on his.

He smiled almost imperceptibly. "Since you're not going to help me help you, I'll go rummage about the kitchen the best I can. In the meantime, sit down," he said, pointing to the sofa.

Brooke, clutching her box of tissues, grudgingly obeyed. "There's English tea on the bottom shelf to the right of the stove."

"English tea," he said, quirking the corner of his mouth in disdain. "I should have known."

With chagrin, she settled into the sofa. As she luxuriated in the warmth of the fire, she listened to his footsteps in the kitchen. Then he began to sing, at first softly, then more loudly.

Brooke leaned an ear toward the kitchen. His rich baritone was surprisingly good.

"The singing doctor!" she said in surprise.

He appeared in the doorway wearing a crooked grin. "You said I needed to improve my bedside manner."

Brooke answered with a sneeze.

He disappeared into the kitchen and returned with a tray, singing all the while.

He set the tray on the coffee table, and removed two steaming mugs of tea and slices of buttered toast. "Feed a cold, starve a fever," he said, sitting on the other end of the sofa. He gave the knot of his tie a tug and crossed one long leg over the other.

"I thought that was an old wives' tale," she said.

"Give the old wives some credit. There's really something to it." The light of the fire danced along his well-chiseled jaw, making Brooke wish he weren't so pleasant to look at. "I'll stay until you finish your toast," he said.

"Trusting soul, aren't you?" she asked.

His lips tightened in a half smile.

She picked up a piece of toast and nibbled casually at the corner. "What do you do when you get sick?"

"I don't get sick," he said earnestly. "I can't let it happen."

Brooke looked at him in disbelief. "Really, now."

"Really," he said, without a blink of an eye. His gaze lingered on her for a moment, making her blood stir. He suddenly diverted his eyes to his mug, and for a moment, an awkward silence hung between them.

The Biggest Heart in Choctaw Hollow 93

That evening, it seemed to Brooke, they had been playing a game—a game of avoidance. The casual chatter and the singing had overlaid thoughts of the kiss they'd shared. Both of them were acting as if it had never happened, as if they were the most casual of friends. Perhaps, she thought painfully, they both knew that for people of vastly different goals, it was best to maintain a reasonable distance.

Brooke quickly finished her toast, although she couldn't taste any of it. "I hardly expected a house call. It was very nice of you to help with the wood," she said.

"It was nothing." He reached over and touched her forehead with the back of his hand. It lingered there for a moment, making her skin tingle. "Stay in bed as much as possible. I'll bring in the extra blanket, then unload the rest of the firewood."

She watched from the front door as Drew stacked the rest of the wood neatly on the porch. Then he stepped back inside and handed her a heavy woolen blanket. In the strong light of a nearby lamp, his face was drawn with fatigue. Brooke felt a twinge of guilt.

"Sleep tight," he said.

"You should take your own advice," she responded, stifling another sneeze.

He lingered in the doorway a moment, as if he had something to say. But suddenly he turned and was gone.

When Brooke awoke, the first thing she became conscious of was her stuffy nose and aching head. She gingerly got out of bed and raised the shade to expose a leaden sky. It was again cold in the cabin and she quickly put on jeans, a turtleneck, and an oversize red wool sweater. She went to the porch and picked up several split logs, surprised at the weight of them. Drew had made it look almost effortless. She piled a stack of them in the fireplace and soon had a nice fire going.

She had settled in front of the fireplace with a hot cup of tea cradled in her hands, when there was a tap on the door. She opened the roughly hewn pine door to find Jessie Johnico standing on the front porch. She held a brown paper bag in both hands.

"Special delivery for a girl with a cold." Her dark eyes crinkled as she smiled.

Brooke felt a pang of surprise. "Come in, Jessie," she said, holding open the sagging screen door. Then, she held out a palm in a cautioning gesture. "On second thought, you should keep your distance. I don't want you to get sick, too."

Jessie gave the air a swat. "Listen, honey. I've had everything there is to have in the way of colds. When you've raised kids like I have, you build up your resistance. Now I've got Thaney. He gets his little bugs now and then, but they don't bother me at all."

She stepped past Brooke, set the bag on the kitchen cabinet, and removed a plastic container. "This is my special homemade soup," she said. "It has cured many folks under the weather. Dr. Griffin said you were to eat all of it."

Brooke was momentarily stunned into silence. "Thank you, Jessie. This is very nice of you," she

The Biggest Heart in Choctaw Hollow   95

finally managed to say. "There was no need to go to this trouble."

"Listen, here," she said with an easy smile. "I always got something going on the stove."

"Jessie, I have some tea made," Brooke offered. "I'd like it if you'd have some with me."

"I suppose I can," she said, sitting at the little kitchen table. "When you have a little mite like Thaney around, a body's got to keep her strength up just to keep up with him. I just got back from taking him to a Cub Scout meeting. They're doing knots today."

Brooke poured Jessie a mug of tea and sat across from her. "Jessie, Thaney has a lot of artistic talent. I'd like to work with him individually to help him cultivate it."

The older woman nodded knowingly. "He's something, isn't he? I'm barely able to keep him in crayons. It's just that I can't afford art lessons."

"No, Jessie. It wouldn't cost anything," she insisted. "It would be my pleasure to work with a child of his ability."

"I sure would appreciate it," she said. "He lost his parents a year ago—a car accident. The drawing is good for him." She took a sip of tea. "Are you feeling any better, honey?"

Brooke nodded.

"The doctor said to remind you to get plenty of rest. He said maybe you'd pay more attention to me than to him."

Brooke smiled softly.

"He's a sweet thing, isn't he?" the older woman asked, not waiting for an answer. "Good-looking, too.

I heard of young ladies pretending to be sick just to get in to see him. Since what happened a couple of years ago, I suppose he's a little gun-shy when it comes to women, and I can't blame him." Her tone rang with a mother's protectiveness.

Brooke leaned forward, eagerly anticipating the rest. But instead of continuing, Jessie glanced at her watch, then set down her mug with a thump. "Oh, dear," she said, jumping up. "I was supposed to have picked up Thaney ten minutes ago."

She patted Brooke on the shoulder. "Honey, I'm just down the road. Call me if you need me and I'll come running."

The screen slapped shut and she was gone.

Sunday came and went with Jessie's hurried delivery of homemade chicken pot pie. On her way to the Indian Methodist Church, she left almost as suddenly as she arrived. She was running late and it was her turn to fire up the church furnace.

In the meantime, the mysterious story that Jessie had never finished dogged Brooke all day. She tried to tell herself that it shouldn't be any of her concern, but she couldn't squelch her yearning to know.

Later in the day, Drew called. The sound of his voice warmed her.

"I'm glad you feel better," he said. "You sound better."

"You sound tired," she responded.

"I am."

"Don't come over."

On Wednesday, after she was well enough to return

to school, he called to ask if she would come in and cancel his Thursday appointments. He wasn't feeling well. Her heart thumped. It was a grand admission for a man who claimed he never got sick.

When she got to the clinic, there was a "closed" sign on the door. Inside, there was no sign of Drew. She tapped on the door of his living quarters.

"It's me, Brooke," she called.

"Come in," a stuffy voice responded.

She found him in the bedroom, sitting up in bed and leaning against several pillows. His arms were crossed over his bare chest, the quilt was pulled up to his elbows, and he wore a look of pure chagrin.

"Thanks for the cold," he said raspily.

Brooke placed her fingers over her mouth and her heart lurched in sympathy. "Oh, Drew," she said, her gaze sweeping over him. He looked miserable without looking miserable, if that were possible, she thought. He was undeniably appealing despite his red nose and watery, tired eyes.

"Odds are I'll live," he said dryly.

"Let me get you something," she said. She was finding it difficult to keep her eyes off his bare, broad chest.

"There's orange juice in the refrigerator. I've already taken my self-prescribed aspirin."

"I'll have it in a second," she said, hurrying out.

Once out of the room, she took a deep breath. How could this cantankerous man be having such an affect on her?

It took more than a second to find the juice. It was jammed behind odds and ends of leftover fast food meals and other exotica. She winced at the jar of pickled pigs' feet and the bag of licorice. She poured the juice in a glass.

"I thought you never got sick," she said, handing it to him.

His bottom lip jutted out in obvious annoyance. Ignoring her, he took a drink.

"You should eat more healthfully," she said. "Throw out those disgusting pigs' feet and that awful candy."

He cocked his head. "Is that the way to talk to a sick man?"

Brooke crossed her arms defensively over her chest. "I'm trying to help make you well."

A corner of his mouth quirked upward. "If you really want to know how I got infected, it probably wasn't from casual contact. It was probably because I kissed you."

Brooke's heart tripped as her eyes riveted on his. "I'm sorry," she said weakly.

He smiled a little. "You're forgiven. Much worse things have happened."

"I should start making phone calls now," she said awkwardly. "Get some rest."

She returned about twenty minutes later and found Drew poring over a medical journal. There were several other medical magazines strewn over the bed. He looked up at her guiltily.

"You're resting, I see." Her voice was tinged with irony.

"Would you like to hear about the latest in sutures?" he asked.

"Have you eaten anything today?" she asked, ignoring the question.

"I didn't feel like it," he grumbled.

Brooke shook her head. "You're terrible. I'll make a decent patient out of you, yet."

She found a can of chicken noodle soup in the kitchen and quickly heated it. She filled a large bowl and took it into the bedroom. But as she approached the bed, she saw him lying on his side, asleep. His hair fell over his brow and his lips were parted slightly. She quietly set the bowl down on a small table next to the bed and stood over him for a moment, watching his chest softly rise and fall. Her gaze followed the line of his unshaven jaw and it took much of her willpower to avoid touching his cheek. She turned out the light and walked softly away. She realized then that when she left Choctaw Hollow, she was going to miss this man very much.

Chapter Seven

"Miss Adler?"

Brooke, wearing a smock smudged with finger paints, turned to find Mr. Krauthammer, the superintendent, in the hallway behind her.

"Can I talk to you?" he asked. "We've got a problem."

Her stomach tightened. "Certainly."

She followed him to a small room adjoining the principal's office and nervously sat across from him.

He took a deep breath. "Some of the parents have complained about the art fees they're having to pay. Cold weather is coming and they don't have the money to buy their kids winter coats, let alone art supplies."

A wave of dismay swept over her. "There must be something we can do," she said.

He shook his head slowly. "The school is already

subsidizing some of the costs. There have been some unforeseen expenses this year and I'm afraid there's just no more money. About half the children haven't paid their fees, and after supplies run out, there won't be any money for more."

Brooke swallowed hard. "But all the children seem to enjoy the art classes. I don't want to turn anyone away."

"Some of these parents have a lot of pride, mainly because they haven't got much else," he continued, strumming his fingers on the table. "They'll pull their children out of the classes before they'll accept charity. And as I've said before, some of them consider art a frill, something that isn't really necessary."

A sick feeling spread through her. She wasn't expecting such sentiments, but she understood why some parents would feel the way they did. Yet if only they could see the light in their children's eyes when they worked on their projects.

She thought for a moment, then announced: "I'll furnish the supplies for everyone," she said, "even for those who can afford to pay. That way, everyone will be treated equally."

The superintendent raised his eyebrows. "We're talking about several hundred dollars."

"I'll manage it," she said.

"I'm sure your family could," he said tentatively.

"I will do this myself," she said firmly.

The day also brought the news that her car was at last repaired. It had taken a week longer than expected. But as she drove after school to pick it up, her excitement was overshadowed by what Mr. Krauthammer had said about some of the children's lack of winter coats. Drew had been right. She was navigating a different world.

The Miata looked beautiful. Frank Harjo had not only repaired the fender and the wheel but had washed it sparkling clean. She made another payment on the repairs and was left with forty dollars. She breathed a sigh of relief. She'd made it through the first month.

She handed over the keys to the truck, slipped behind the wheel of the little red sports car and drove to the clinic.

She tapped on the door of his apartment. There was no response except for the muffled giggle of a youthful female voice. Brooke felt a little jolt of surprise. For a moment, she was unsure of whether to stay or leave, then she tapped louder. In a moment, Jessie appeared at the door. In the background was chatter and laughter.

"Brooke, come in," she said with a smile.

"I just came to check on Drew," she said tentatively.

Jessie laughed. "So has half the town."

She followed her into the kitchen where a dozen women, young and old, stood chattering. Brooke saw counters laden with cakes, pies, casseroles, and containers of homemade soup, and blinked. Over Drew's closed bedroom door was a banner reading, "Get Well, Dr. Griffin."

Jessie took her by the arm and introduced her to everyone. They greeted her warmly.

"How is he?" she finally managed to ask.

"Much better," Jessie said. "He was just worn out.

He has gone nonstop for the last two years. The cold was a blessing in disguise. It forced him to get some rest."

Brooke felt awkward. "Since he's in such good hands, I'll go. And if you like, tell Thaney he's welcome to come over after school tomorrow for some art lessons."

A broad smile crossed Jessie's face. "Oh, he'd love that."

Brooke had just turned to leave when the door to Drew's bedroom opened. As he emerged, dressed in khakis and a faded denim shirt and his face shadowed with two days' growth of beard, some of the visiting ladies sounded a brief cheer. He grinned crookedly, then his eyes settled on Brooke. They were no longer clouded by fatigue, but clear and bright. Her heart gave a little flutter.

He gave the women a little wave and took Brooke by the arm. "I'll be back in the office in the morning. The appointment schedule . . ." he said, leading her into the clinic. He closed the door behind them.

"What about it?" she asked.

"Nothing," he whispered. He was rumpled, bearded, and irresistible. "Save me from all these women before I overdose on their mothering."

Brooke laughed lightly. "They love you, Drew, and they're never going to let you leave Choctaw Hollow."

He touched a tissue to his nose and grinned weakly. "At this point, I don't think they have much to worry about."

* * *

The next afternoon when she got home from school, there was a large and unexpected parcel on the front porch of the cabin. It was wrapped neatly in heavy brown paper and addressed in a familiar hand—a dated, scrolled penmanship that spelled Grandmama. The return address was Willow Boulevard.

Perplexed, Brooke bent to pick it up, but she could barely lift it. She opened the cabin door and dragged it inside. Grandmama was surely up to something.

She tore away the paper and opened the box to find dozens of smaller bundles wrapped in paper. A note with her grandmother's engraved letterhead lay on top.

My Dear Brooke,
The chrysanthemums are the loveliest in years. The fall garden tour was a wonderful success with Willow Boulevard leading the show. I wish you could have seen it.
Hannah made your favorite lasagna yesterday and we all talked about how much we miss you. Ned misses having someone to talk to while he does his woodworking projects.
One of your old school chums—Danielle Kelley—is back in town visiting her parents. She said she's sorry she missed you.
I hope you enjoy the little surprises I sent you. Do write. Hannah and Ned also send their love.
                                                    Grandmama

Brooke felt a twinge of homesickness. She felt a sudden longing for the sweet, earthy scent of the hundreds of chrysanthemums that Ned tended so carefully and for Hannah's lasagna. Choctaw Hollow was two hundred miles from the nearest bulb of Italian cheese. And yes, she missed Ned and Hannah and even Grandmama.

Grandmama, she thought again. She hadn't said a word about her heart. That omission surely had some significance.

Brooke thought guiltily of the old lady as she began to unwrap the parcels. There were dried tomatoes, Greek olives, a wedge of fresh Parmesan, a jar of artichoke hearts, and a package of dried cherries.

Digging farther, she found Swiss chocolate, coconut milk, stalks of lemongrass, a jar of Oriental curry powder, Japanese rice, dried tortellini, and two bottles of French wine. She heaved a heavy sigh. Grandmama had worked her spell again. How wonderful it would be to browse the foreign food shops with Hannah and to be away from the incessant rain and mud.

With the last parcel, a box of English tea, was a note in her grandmother's hand: Filet mignon, packed in dry ice, will be delivered soon.''

Brooke sat cross-legged on the floor and stared into the cold fireplace. She knew she was disappointing her grandmother and that the old lady had much difficulty understanding why she wanted to break free of her upbringing. But as difficult as it was, it was the only way to gain the strength and autonomy that she needed.

She got up, brought in logs from the porch, and started a fire. She was putting the last of the food items away in the kitchen when there was a knock on the door. She hurriedly set the wine on the counter and went to answer it. Thaney and his dog stood on the front porch.

"Granny said I can come over and draw with you." There was an orange soda mustache on his upper lip.

"You certainly can," she said, opening the rusting screen. The dog, wearing a red bandanna, scampered in after him.

Thaney, small for his seven years, went straight for Brooke's easel by the large north window. On it was a sketch of wildflowers in a jar on the windowsill. He peered at it closely, leaving smudged fingerprints on the bottom. "You can draw a lot better than my granny," he announced.

Brooke smiled. "Your granny cooks much better than I do."

"Yeah, she sure is a good cooker," he said, picking up a charcoal pencil.

Brooke handed him a sketch pad. "Draw anything you like," she said. "As you draw, I'll show you some new things."

He plopped on the sofa and sat forward slightly. "I'm going to draw Dog," he said, his large brown eyes sparkling.

Dog lay curled up beside the easel.

Brooke sat beside him and watched as the pencil moved in his chubby fist. A form began to take shape and Brooke's earlier assessment of his ability was confirmed. He was a natural. The proportions of head to body were right and the boy had an amazing eye for detail. He didn't have the coordination or experience to create a perfect sketch, but for his age, she found his attempt remarkable.

She showed him how to add depth and shadow and helped him draw the dog's fur.

"Wow!" he exclaimed, holding it up. "I'm going to hang this in Dog's dog house. I'm fixing it up," he explained. "I put some carpet in it and Granny's going to make him his own pillow."

Brooke gave the boy a little hug. "Dog is lucky to have you. And today, Thaney, you've done very good work."

The boy grinned shyly.

They were interrupted by a knock on the door. This time, it was Jessie.

"I've come to pick up that boy of mine," she said with a knowing smile. "I was afraid that once he started drawing, he might not want to come home."

Thaney jumped up and ran toward her, waving the drawing. "Look what I did!"

Jessie shook her head. "Why, haven't I seen that dog somewhere before? That looks just like Dog," she said, directing a wink at Brooke.

"It is Dog," Thaney interjected.

"I hope he's not too much trouble," Jessie said apologetically.

"Not at all," Brooke said, shaking her head. "He's quite a little artist."

"He sure didn't get it from me," she said with a laugh. She reached down and gave Dog a pat on the head. "In the process, did you get the complete history of Dog?"

Brooke smiled and shook her head.

"Dr. Griffin brought him by last winter. He'd found him when he was out making a medical call. The poor little thing was half frozen and half starved. He didn't have a place for him and I guess he figured I couldn't say no," she said with a laugh.

Brooke's insides stirred at the mention of Drew's name. "I hope he's feeling all right today," she said.

"I talked to my friend Opal Carnahan this morning and she said he's doing fine and seeing patients. She checked on him on her way to the grocery store."

"The people of Choctaw Hollow certainly take good care of him," Brooke remarked.

"He takes care of us," Jessie said simply. "There are people who would have died if it hadn't been for him. I'm just afraid he keeps to himself too much. Whether he'll admit it or not, he needs a wife. I'd just hate it if Cheryl Padgett turned him sour on women altogether.

Brooke's heart gave a hard thump. "Sour?" she murmured.

"They were engaged, childhood sweethearts." Jessie explained briefly. "Cheryl broke it off."

Brooke stood stone still. A weight seemed to settle in her stomach.

After a moment of silence, Jessie turned and took Thaney by the hand. "Come on, Norman Rockwell. It's suppertime."

Grudgingly, the little boy got up. "Can I come back, Miss Adler?"

"Of course you can," she said, "anytime you like."

"Careful," his grandmother said with a chuckle, "or you'll end up with a permanent houseguest."

After Jessie saw that Thaney had thanked Brooke

properly, they were gone, leaving her alone with her thoughts about Drew and her own painful memories of a heart once broken.

On Friday, she worked an hour overtime at the clinic. There was a broken toe, a case of colic, a spider bite, a persistently sore throat, ringworm, and a case of anemia. There was little blood to see except for a finger stick for a six-year-old girl. Brooke helped Drew get the little girl through it by drawing a quick cartoon of a brave girl and a crying doctor.

They scarcely had a chance to speak to each other until all the patients were gone.

"Thanks again for the cartoon trick," he said, pulling his stethoscope from around his neck. As he took off his coat, she could not help but admire the squareness of his shoulders. "How am I going to manage without you once May rolls around?"

She looked into his blue-gray eyes and her heart seemed to droop. "You managed without me before, didn't you?" she finally managed to say.

"I suppose I did." His tone was irritatingly detached.

There was a strum of disappointment from deep within her heart. She tried to hide it behind a false smile. She fumbled aimlessly with the papers on her desk. "Speaking of management, I've been meaning to talk to you about your office system," she said. "All this should be computerized, you know."

He gave a nod and sat on the corner of her desk. His familiar spicy scent made her blood rush. "It isn't computerized because Mrs. Jackson wasn't comfortable with technology. She wouldn't even use an electric typewriter until I forced her to. I had to take the manual out and hide it."

Brooke's brows rose in surprise.

"After all," Drew continued with a shrug of his broad shoulders, "she was seventy-two years old. She'd been working for doctors since she got out of high school and things were just fine the way she'd always done them. She said she didn't want to risk a hard day's work evaporating in a power surge, that she'd take her pencil and ledger any day. And that's the way it was," he said with a little smile. "She ran the office and I tended to the patients. That was our little understanding."

"I could help get a computer system set up," she offered. "It would be a big help with record-keeping and billing."

He looked at her with narrowed eyes. "You wouldn't mind? It would involve some extra time, you know."

"It would help you," she said. She hesitated for a moment. "After I'm gone."

Drew rose to his feet and without looking at her stroked his jaw for a moment. "All right then," he said stiffly.

Brooke finished straightening up the desk and got up. She threw on her red cashmere blazer over jeans and a white cotton shirt. As she glanced up, Drew was studying her. Her cheeks warmed. He diverted his gaze.

"Good night, Brooke," he said. His voice almost

echoed in the empty room that she realized was essentially his life.

A brief pause followed. "Drew," she said, "my grandmother sent me sort of a care package the other day. There are ingredients there for a great meal but I don't have anyone to share it with. I'd like for you to come over Sunday—about one if you're not busy. At least let me make it up to you for giving you that awful cold."

A little smile touched his lips. "I don't hold that against you, but I'll accept your invitation just the same."

It was raining when Drew arrived. Droplets of water glistened in his hair and on his shoulders as he stood on the porch. With a lopsided grin that reminded Brooke of a shy schoolboy, he handed her a bouquet of mixed flowers.

"How nice of you," she said.

"I can be nice once in a while."

He sat on the porch railing, unlaced his muddy hiking boots, and placed them on a piece of newspaper next to Brooke's. "It looks like you're getting the hang of mountain living," he said.

She gave him a chiding look. "I'm not doing badly and you know it," she said. "You just won't admit it."

He followed her into the kitchen, where she set the flowers in a blue and white Chinese porcelain vase she'd brought from the city. She studied the flowers for a moment, then rearranged some of the stems. She looked up to find a gleam of irony in his eyes.

"That's a nice, rustic vase," he said. "Every mountain cabin should have one."

She gave him a look of impatience. "It's not from the Ming Dynasty or anything."

The corners of his mouth lifted into a little smile. "I suppose not."

"Perhaps you'd like a glass of wine," she offered.

"It would be nice," he said.

She handed him one of the bottles that Grandmama had sent her, along with a corkscrew. He studied the label for a moment, then glanced at her, his expression unreadable. He deftly removed the cork with a resounding pop. He partially filled two crystal glasses that Brooke had set on the counter.

"To an end to the rain," he said, raising his glass.

But at the moment she touched her glass to his, a rumble of thunder sounded, followed by a driving downpour.

They hurried to the large north window to find the rain dashing against the panes.

Drew's expression was troubled. "If there's much more of this, the river will be up over its banks," he said. "Butter Creek, being a tributary, could flood as well."

Brooke's stomach tightened. The meandering creek, which had been included in several of her sketches, was hardly more than a stone's throw from the cabin.

He turned toward her and placed a hand on her elbow. "Enough about rain. Did I ever tell you about the time I delivered a baby in a circus tent?"

Brooke looked at him warily.

The Biggest Heart in Choctaw Hollow   113

He led her to the sofa. He sat across from her in an old wicker rocker. He stretched out his legs and crossed his ankles. He was dressed casually in jeans, a plaid shirt, and a dark gray rag wool sweater. The light from the fireplace gave his brown hair a rich burnished look.

"It was a warm, clear summer night. It was my first month of practice in Choctaw Hollow and the circus had come to town. The wife of the clown, who had some sort of act involving poodles doing tricks—playing guitars and such—had gone into labor and everything was happening so fast that they didn't have time to get her to a hospital. By the time I got there, the baby had already crowned. A few minutes later, he was born under the trapeze, while his mother wore a rhinestone tiara. So you see, Choctaw Hollow is not always dull or wet."

Brooke laughed softly. "Is there any entertainment besides the circus?"

He toyed with the stem of his wineglass. "There's no symphony, opera, or ballet, of course, but there are the Saturday night dances at the American Legion hall, a rodeo every summer, and high school sports. The schools stage plays and operettas now and then." His expression clouded. "I'm afraid that wouldn't entice many people to stay here."

Brooke gave a rueful nod. "For a lot of doctors, this would be a hardship post, but it doesn't seem that way for you."

He stared into his glass for a moment. "When I was fourteen, my younger brother died of leukemia." A pained expression crossed his handsome face. "My mother was a widow and we had no health insurance. This town rallied around her even though most people had as little or less than we did. Money was raised in all sorts of ways to help pay for some experimental treatment for him. Of course, it failed, but I've never forgotten what people did for us. It was then that I got interested in medicine and started spending a lot of time with old Doc Murphy. You know the rest."

His words triggered an ache deep inside her chest.

"It was at that age that I also began getting some cold splashes of reality," she said. "Until then, my biggest disappointment had been my failure to make the swim team at the all-girls school I attended."

Brooke sketchily and hastily mentioned her mother's spiraling depression and other family problems. Pained by the memories, she rose so abruptly that Drew's eyes widened.

"Grandmama had some wonderful filets mignons sent," she said. "Come help me make them."

As Brooke browned a layer of salt in the bottom of a cast-iron skillet, Drew leaned against the refrigerator with his arms folded across his chest and watched with interest. "Where did you learn that? Surely they don't teach cooking at an exclusive girls school."

"I learned it from Hannah, our maid," she explained, pounding cracked peppercorns into the steaks. "It's really very simple."

He smiled faintly.

"Grandmama, like all girls of her era, was only taught how to make a good pot of tea and to serve it just right to the guests. Other than that, she barely knows the way to the kitchen. Of course, she thought

I should be out socializing instead of hanging around the hired help. But," she added with a shrug, "they seemed more interesting. Ned told stories about growing up in Scotland and Hannah taught me all sorts of interesting things about food."

She placed the steaks in the skillet and looked up to find him studying her closely. His expression was thoughtful.

"Brooke, what are your plans after leaving here?"

Her eyes linked to his and she felt an odd little twinge in her heart. "Every artist wants to create, of course, but we have to figure out ways to support ourselves while doing it. So I hope to find work in a museum or a gallery."

"Have you had any second thoughts about the agreement you made with your grandmother?" he asked.

"No," she said. "If there are any regrets, it's that I'm hurting her. But don't get the idea that I'm terribly brave, because I'm not. It's just that past events have driven me, that's all. I want to be loved for me, not the family bank account. I want to succeed because of my own efforts, not because of who I am."

After she turned over the steaks, Drew put his arms around her waist and gently pulled her away from the stove. He drew her into his embrace, his warm yet gentle strength leaving her almost breathless. Her heart pounded against the firm muscles of his chest. He lowered his head to kiss her. Just as she parted her lips to meet his, there was a knock on the front door.

Chapter Eight

Brooke stiffened as if she'd been jolted from a sweetly pleasant dream. Drew pulled back from her, his eyes murky with longing. A frown formed on his lips. His arms dropped to his sides.

"You'd better see who it is," he said huskily.

With weak knees and clouded senses and her heart still thundering in her chest, Brooke opened the front door to find Thaney and Dog. Thaney, his feet covered with mud, pulled a piece of rolled paper out from the folds of his Superman cape. "Can I show you what I drawed?"

Brooke, her blood still tingling, relented. "Of course," she said, taking the drawing. "Don't forget to leave your shoes on the porch."

The child stepped out of them and entered, followed by Dog. Brooke turned to find Drew standing a few

The Biggest Heart in Choctaw Hollow 117

feet behind her with his hands in his pockets. The corners of his mouth tipped upwards in a little smile.

"Dr. Drew!" the boy shrilled, striding toward him.

Drew pulled the child to him and tousled his straight, shiny black hair. "How's it going, my man?" Dog's wagging tail thumped against the floor.

"Fine. Is Miss Adler sick?"

Drew gave a low, gentle laugh. "You'll have to ask her how she's feeling." His eyes, their blue turned dusky and full of meaning, connected with hers.

Her blood stirred. She diverted her gaze to the boy. "Dr. Drew is just here for a visit," she said, dodging the question.

Brooke unfurled the paper to find a picture of the little yellow Johnico house with Butter Creek meandering nearby. In one window was Thaney, looking out. In another was Dog. It was sketched, then colored with crayon with impressive accuracy. "Oh, Thaney," she exclaimed, "this is so charming."

He beamed proudly. "It's for you."

Suddenly, she felt the warmth of Drew's body as he looked over her shoulder. For a moment, she lost her voice. "I'm very happy to have it," she finally managed to say. "Thank you." She bent over and kissed the boy on the crown.

"Good work, Superman," Drew said.

The boy's smile broadened, then he glanced into the kitchen. "Something sure smells good," he said. "It's making me hungry."

Brooke looked into the boy's liquid brown eyes and her heart turned soft. She still felt the tingle from

Drew's embrace and it frightened her. She needed a distracting presence and that was Thaney. "There's plenty for all of us," she said. "Come sit down."

Brooke gave Drew a glance of apology. He responded with an understanding smile.

They sat down at the little kitchen table which Brooke had covered with a cutwork cloth. She gave portions of her steak, twice-baked potatoes, and salad to the little boy. He ate with relish, giving a bite or two to the dog.

"This must be the only dog in Choctaw Hollow to ever sample filet mignon," Drew said.

Thaney gave the tines of his fork a lick. "My mom worked at the Green Tomato," he said. "She used to get to bring leftovers home, but there wasn't any of this." A fleeting sadness crossed his face, bringing an ache to Brooke's chest.

Abruptly, the boy placed an elbow on the table and propped up his chin. He looked at Brooke suspiciously, then Drew. "Is Miss Adler your girlfriend?"

Drew blinked. Brooke felt her cheeks redden.

"Would you like for her to be?" Drew asked obliquely.

"No," he said, shaking his dark bangs. "I want her to be my girlfriend."

Brooke grinned. "Don't you think I'm a little old for you?"

He shook his head adamantly. "Do you like him?" he asked, pointing at Drew.

She felt Drew's eyes on her and cringed. It was a question to which she herself had been dodging the answer.

"Would you like a cherry tart?" she asked in an attempt to distract him.

His eyes widened. "Yeah!"

Thankful for children's short attention spans, she quickly cleared the table and brought out the tarts that she'd made from the dried cherries. On each she put a dollop of whipped cream. She set one in front of the boy. When she served Drew, his eyes met hers in a flash of guarded intensity that left her off balance.

Thaney, forgetting about Drew and Brooke, lost himself in his dessert. The room was awkwardly quiet except for the occasional scratchings of Dog and the clinking of forks against plates. Suddenly, Thaney looked out the window where dusk was rapidly falling and jumped up. "Uh-oh," he said. "I'm supposed to be home before dark."

After thanking Brooke for the meal, he tore out the front door, leaving in his wake a beating silence. Drew was the first to break it.

"I thought teachers were supposed to answer children's questions," he said.

She bit her thumb. "To children that age, liking someone of the opposite sex means the same thing as loving them."

"I see." There was a sparkle in his eyes. "We certainly wouldn't want to give the boy the impression that ours is a mutual admiration society, would we?"

Brooke shot him a look of annoyance. "Speaking of Thaney, why don't you let me display his work and the work of the other children in the clinic? We can hang it on the walls in the waiting—"

"You're very deft at changing subjects, aren't

you?'' he interrupted. "To answer your question, I like the idea very much." His gaze lingered. "It would be something good to continue after you're gone."

She swallowed hard. "Yes, it would."

A muscle in his jaw twitched. "Where would you like to go when your job here is over?"

"I always had a dream of working in Chicago, New York, or Los Angeles, or even Santa Fe," she said. "If you want to do gallery or museum work and maintain contacts, it's almost essential to be in or near the art centers. I'm going to be on my own, you know. My success is going to depend partly on geography."

He looked at her intently, his expression controlled.

The memory of his closeness sent odd sensations dancing through her and she suddenly experienced a sense of loss.

"I'll know where to find you," she said, feigning a lightness she didn't feel.

"It looks like I'm here to stay," he said with a shrug. "It's part of me, Brooke. I'm needed here and I'm appreciated. Without me, there would be no doctor within a fifty-mile radius."

"I understand," she said, "and I admire you."

He smiled lightly. "The admiration is not necessary, but the understanding is appreciated." He studied her face for a moment, his expression unreadable. "I know there's not much to keep people here. People follow their dreams, wherever they may lead. That's something I've learned to accept."

He took a deep breath and stepped away from the table as if trying to distance himself from an unpleasant memory. She rose and followed. He strolled over

The Biggest Heart in Choctaw Hollow

to her easel and studied a pen and ink drawing Brooke had done of the mountain view outside the window.

"You know," he said, turning toward her, "I keep thinking that with one more mishap or one more gully washer, you'll be gone."

An old resentment rose in her chest. "You can think whatever you like," she said, shooting him a look of defiance. "But I've always finished what I've started."

Looking at her with a mysterious gleam in his eyes, he grasped her shoulders and pulled her to him. His face was within inches of hers. "I also finish what I start."

He cupped her cheeks in his hands and kissed her lightly. Then he pulled her against him and kissed her again, this time with conviction. The heat of his touch burned into her cheeks and her heart beat wildly. Suddenly, he released her, leaving her dazed and breathless.

"American Indians and the Irish have a similar expression," he said. "When parting, they say, 'May the wind be always at your back.' You and I always have to keep in mind," he said, "that we're going to have to say good-bye. For us, there's no future, only now. Let's try not to take things too seriously and enjoy it. If you're not sure you even like me, all the better." With that, he added a casual buss on the cheek.

November arrived in a cold rainstorm with whipping winds. Bright bursts of autumn foliage which drew tourists from miles around were being carried away in the gusts. Left behind were bare branches, the foreboding of a long winter, and disappointed mountain residents who hoped to benefit from the seasonal rush of buses that carried tourists over the spiraling mountain highway to view the foliage.

The weather matched Brooke's gloomy mood. The children were doing well in their art classes and she took pleasure in their enthusiasm. Her meager finances were getting back in order and she found satisfaction in helping Drew at the clinic. Grandmama was at an affair of the Daughters of the American Revolution in Virginia, her aches and pains momentarily forgotten, and Brooke's telephone remained blissfully silent. But there was a heaviness in her heart that she couldn't shake.

It had to do with Drew. There was the apparent ease at which he could hold her in his arms, then let her go, as if feelings had a switch. They had no future together, he'd said, only the present. She had to concede that he was right, but he seemed to be taking it in stride.

The trouble was that the memory of his kisses still burned on her lips. If only she could dismiss it as easily as he seemed to. And to make it worse, he seemed to sense how she felt.

Their work together reverted to being crisply professional as the workload grew heavier. Cooler weather brought more illnesses, filling the waiting room. There was another round of layoffs at the timber mill because of the continued rains. Some of the medical bills went unpaid or paid in meager installments.

Brooke had sent off for frames for student artwork and the pictures now lined the walls of the waiting

The Biggest Heart in Choctaw Hollow 123

room. They were pictures of the mountains, of their families, or of "Dr. Drew" at work. She was pleasantly surprised at the attention they got.

She'd contacted some of her friends in the Junior Assistance League for help in gathering up several dozen children's coats, outgrown by their previous owners but in good condition.

She'd gotten a computer system installed in the office.

Before she knew it, Thanksgiving had arrived. She spent the day with Jessie and Thaney while Drew spent most of the week in Dallas at a medical workshop.

A few days after the holiday, a large box arrived at the clinic.

"What have we here?" Drew asked at the end of a long schedule of appointments. "Another care package from Grandmama? Let me guess," he said, his eyes suddenly alight with amusement. "Truffles, foie gras, a couple of wheels of French cheese?"

Miffed, she glared at him. "For your information, these are winter coats for some of your little patients. If they're not patients now, they might be without warm clothing."

His brows lifted slightly in surprise. "A thoughtful idea," he said, stepping behind her desk, where the box sat.

Brooke handed him a box opener from her desk drawer and he cut through the seal. He turned back the flaps and pulled out a small red coat with a hood. He examined it front and back. "Like new," he said, obviously pleased. "How did you manage this?"

"With a little help from a few pampered and spoiled socialites like myself." Her voice rang with irony.

His mouth quirked into a little smile. "How do you plan to distribute them?"

"I have a plan," she said. "The teachers know who needs the coats. I'll send notes to the parents. Perhaps we can hang some coats in the clinic and the people who need them can take them. I'll put them in the entry so they won't be seen taking them, if that makes them uncomfortable."

Drew looked thoughtfully at the ceiling while stroking his jaw. "We can give it a try."

"A try?" Perplexed, she walked out from behind her desk. "I don't understand."

"For some people, taking charity hurts their pride," he said, his voice softening. His eyes lingered on her face, sending little prickles up her spine.

"You mean they would rather their children do without than take charity?" She felt a surge of indignation.

"Not really. They just try to solve the problem in another way, that's all."

Brooke gazed at him in bewilderment. "Choctaw Hollow is a hard place to understand," she said.

His blue-gray gaze darkened. "It can be to outsiders," he said.

Her lips tightened. "I guess you're reminding me that I'm out of my element."

He looked at her thoughtfully, then reached down and gave her chin a gentle tweak. "Out of your element, maybe, but your heart's in the right place. Hang up a few coats and we'll see what happens."

The coats hung in the entry for a week before one was finally taken. Of the dozen or so notes sent to parents, there were only two responses.

"I just don't understand," Brooke lamented. She'd stopped at the clinic at closing time. Although it was past six, Drew was just eating "lunch"—fried chicken from the Green Tomato Café. He wore a blue scrub suit and thick woolen socks, but no shoes. Looking annoyingly desirable despite his rumpled state, he offered her a chicken wing from his plate. She took it, then sat across from him at his small dining room table. There was something about his Spartan existence that touched her. She'd known dozens of young doctors' wives whose husbands were socially ambitious. Drew's life contrasted sharply with theirs.

"I think you need to change your strategy," he said finally.

She looked at him quizzically. "How?"

He pushed his plate away and leaned forward. "Put yourself in the shoes of someone with exceptional pride."

Brooke sighed in exasperation. "Drew, this is your territory. Help me figure this out."

A stubborn crinkle appeared in his chin. "You figure it out."

Brooke stood up abruptly, waving her barely nibbled chicken wing at him. "Do you know what? I think you're enjoying seeing me 'out of my element,' as you call it. Go ahead. Have a good time."

The tinge of amusement on his face made her nerves itch with perturbance. Striding toward the door, she stopped halfway, pivoted on her heel, then deposited the wing on his plate. "Here," she grumbled, "you can have your chicken back."

Not giving him the satisfaction of seeing the smile that was surely on his face, she strode out of the clinic.

Brooke went back to the cabin and plopped on the sofa, her arms folded across her chest. She might as well be in a foreign country, she thought, for all she knew about the mountain mentality. If it rained much more, everyone would be needing life jackets instead. They'd probably even refuse those. How, she grumbled, now pacing the floor, could Drew spend his life here?

She ran her fingers through her hair and sighed deeply. She couldn't allow good coats to be lying in a box when there were children who needed them. Drew, of all people, should be able to see that.

She suddenly realized the cabin was stone cold. She brought in several heavy logs from the porch and dropped them onto the hearth. With difficulty, because of the damp wood, she finally got a fire going.

Then, a fire seemed to ignite in her mind as well. People would pay for the coats if they had money, but since they had none, perhaps they would take them in trade. She grabbed a sketch pad and began to take notes. For each coat, she could trade a rick of wood, a dozen homemade biscuits, or repair work at the school. They would also be free to make their own offers.

The next day, she arranged for notes to be sent home with students. Within days, every coat was gone.

Eager to share her delight with Drew and to let him know that she had managed after all, she stopped by the clinic, but he was gone. No one at the Green Tomato had seen him that evening. Disappointed, she went home.

At nine o'clock that night, she called him, but there was no answer, nor was there an answer at nine-thirty. She'd given up and had begun to prepare for bed when there was a knock on the door. She threw on her terrycloth robe and peered through the window to find Drew's Jeep parked outside. Her heart gave a little lurch. She opened the door to find him holding a small wooden box.

"Am I still welcome here?" he asked, his neat eyebrows poised in uncertainty.

Brooke pulled her robe together at the neck and without saying anything, opened the screen.

"I suppose this means yes," he said, his gaze sweeping over her bare legs.

Self-consciously, she stepped back and folded her arms over her chest. "What brings you here so late in the evening?" she asked.

He grinned that rare crooked smile that stirred something in her veins. There was a dark smudge on one cheek and his hair was damp. "I didn't intend for it to be this late and for that, I apologize. I've come by to give you this." He handed her a small cardboard box. "I would have wrapped it, but I'm not very good with bows and things."

Brooke gazed at him in surprise.

"Well, aren't you going to open it?" he asked. "For that matter, aren't you going to ask me to sit down? Aren't you going to offer me something hot to drink? I haven't had the best of nights, you know."

She frowned. "Please sit. Would you care for some hot chocolate?"

Drew sat in the old rocker and crossed his long legs. "Thank you," he said, his eyes filled with mirth. "Some hot chocolate would be very nice. But first, open the box."

Brooke sat on the sofa and lifted off the lid. Inside was a miniature wooden chest with a mountain scene carved on the top. She opened it to find it fragrant with the scent of cedar. "This is wonderful," she said. "It's hand carved."

"Mr. Isherwood makes them in his spare time, which he happens to have a lot of since he's seventy-six years old," Drew explained. "Part of the process of buying a cedar box from Mr. Isherwood is sitting with him while he whittles. And the stories," Drew said with a sigh. "Tonight, while he added the finishing touches on that box, I heard about the great possum shortage during the Depression. A fascinating tale, no pun intended. Remind me to tell you sometime. And then, to make my journey to Mr. Isherwood's more time-consuming, I managed to have a flat. It's hard to jack up a car in the mud, you know."

Brooke felt a pang of guilt. "I'm sorry. I appreciate the box very much, but I'm not sure I was worth all that trouble."

"It's just my way of congratulating you on solving the coat problem," he said, his eyes filled with a quiet pride.

"How did you know?"

"As you said, this is my territory. I'm in tune. Now,

The Biggest Heart in Choctaw Hollow 129

if you don't mind, I'll make myself some hot chocolate," he said, getting up.

Brooke scurried after him and pulled an envelope of drink mix from the cabinet. "I'll make myself useful yet," she said. "You might even miss me when I'm gone."

He took two cups from a shelf and turned toward her. His expression was unreadable. "We'll see." His tone was noncommittal.

Brooke felt a stirring of disappointment. "I'm going home for Christmas, you know. You'll probably hardly notice my absence."

Without looking at her, he poured boiling water into their cups and stirred the contents. As he handed her a cup, she could see that his eyes were clouded.

"Has it occurred to you that you might be taking a chance by going home?" he asked. "Amid all the luxury and familiar surroundings, you may decide that breaking away may not be what you want after all."

Her stomach tightened. "Are you trying to weaken my resolve?"

"No," he said, his gaze penetrating. "I just want what's best for you in the long run."

She glared at him. "I can take care of myself, thank you."

He responded with a mirthful gleam in his eye. "That might be a bigger job than you think."

"Look at you," she said accusatorily. She took a cloth from the counter, moistened it under the faucet, and rubbed the smudge of dirt from his cheek. "You can't even keep yourself clean."

He grabbed the cloth, tossed it into the sink, then

pulled her into his arms. His lips came down on hers with force, hunger, and longing. Answering his need with her own, she slipped her arms around his neck and melted against him.

His fingers caressed the nape of her neck, then moved gently over her shoulders. She gasped as one shoulder of her robe fell away, exposing her bare flesh to his warm touch.

Suddenly, he pulled back, his breath ragged. He kissed her shoulder lightly before covering it with the robe, sending prickles of yearning through her.

"Hot chocolate is somewhat underrated as an aphrodisiac," he said thickly.

Brooke's cheeks tingled as she pulled the lapels of her robe tightly around her throat. She slightly distanced herself from him.

"We were talking about Christmas, weren't we?" She managed an even tone in her voice despite the wild beating of her heart.

"I seem to have forgotten," he said coyly, leaning casually against the cabinet.

"No you haven't. I suppose Christmas is another excuse for the women of Choctaw Hollow to indulge you," she said, trying to ignore the lingering heat on her lips.

"At least they appreciate me," he said. "It usually works like this: I make my rounds at various houses, that way I don't have to turn down anyone's invitation. I eat a little here and a little there and end it at Jessie Johnico's for some of her absolutely perfect pecan pie."

"That's not a proper dinner. It's a foraging spree," she said.

His lopsided grin reappeared. "Call it what you like, but while you're making fussy little toasts with your crystal glasses, I will be having Christmas my way—with a very extended family eating from discount store plates."

She shot him a look of impatience. "Then you won't miss me," she said. "And I certainly won't miss you."

A little smile played on his lips which incensed her even more. It wouldn't have hurt so much if she had been telling the truth.

Chapter Nine

Grandmama was almost faint with joy when Brooke arrived for Christmas. She alternately hugged her granddaughter and fanned herself with a heavily jeweled hand.

"Let me look at you," she said, holding her at arm's length. The old lady's pale blue eyes sparkled with delight. "Darling, it's wonderful to see you, but I do believe that forsaken place has left you a little pale."

"Grandmama, it's good to be home," Brooke said, ignoring the remark. The old woman was, as usual, immaculately coiffed and manicured, and stylishly dressed. But Brooke realized with some alarm that her grandmother had noticeably aged in the few months since she'd been gone. Sadly, she kissed her papery cheek once again.

Hannah and Ned appeared in the hallway with

plenty of hugs and kisses. Brooke felt a lump in her throat. She hadn't realized how much she missed them all.

The house looked beautiful. The windows sparkled in the sunshine and there were wreaths and garlands with red bows everywhere.

"I have a wonderful surprise for you," Grandmama said, sitting in her favorite chair as Hannah went after refreshments.

Brooke sat on the sofa. Its soft cushions contrasted sharply with the hard springs of the cabin couch. "I suppose if I asked what it is, it wouldn't be a surprise."

"I'm giving you a reception Saturday night," she said with obvious pleasure. "As for the rest of the surprise, you'll have to wait."

Christmas came and went in a blur of "company" china, silver, and a dozen of Hannah's wonderful holiday dishes. Brooke basked in the comfort of central heating, got a salon haircut, and went shopping for exotic foods. But her mind was on Drew. She thought of him as she gazed in shop windows and as she drove around the city. Oddly, the familiar sights seemed to have lost some of their lure.

She missed his irreverent wit, his devotion to his patients. Most of all she missed his touch. But she knew it was fruitless to think about it. The window of time they had together was quickly closing. She was aghast at how fast the days were shuttling by and she knew why: She didn't want her time with him to end so soon.

For the reception, which Brooke had been secretly dreading, Grandmama had hired a small chamber orchestra and a caterer. Brooke, dressed simply in a fitted black dress, matching pumps, and a string of pearls, steeled herself for the arrival of Grandmama's friends. From her bedroom window, she watched the driveway fill with expensive cars.

Many were people she'd known all her life. Mixed in were a few strangers. Grandmama flitted from one to another like a bee feasting on the honey of society. Grandmama was indeed in her element.

They greeted Brooke, taking their turns at small talk. "Oh, how quaint," one said of the mountains, "but surely you must die of boredom."

One guest excused himself periodically to chat on his cellular phone in the entryway. "A big deal in the making," he said, making sure others overheard.

She learned the McFarlands had recently planted five thousand dollars worth of imported tulip bulbs and an old friend of Grandmama's was having a terrible time deciding if a certain couple should be recommended for admission to the country club.

Wasn't it terribly hard to get good help these days? an old dowager complained. Brooke must come visit the Eversoles' new house when it was completed. It would have two kitchens, one with two dishwashers. The Paytons, going to Antarctica, lamented that they were running out of exotic destinations.

All the while, Brooke thought of some families' daily struggle to survive in Choctaw Hollow. She'd grown up with such chatter, but tonight she found it especially grating.

The Biggest Heart in Choctaw Hollow   135

She was taking a momentary break at the refreshment table when Grandmama whisked her away. "Now, there's someone I'd really like for you to meet."

She introduced Brooke to Weldon Reed, an older man with a natty pink bow tie and closely cropped silver hair. He took Brooke's hand, bent with a flourish, and kissed it.

"I'm an admirer of your art," he said. "Wonderful watercolors. An innovative use of color, I'd say, both delicate and bold. A very individual style."

Brooke, feeling a flash of surprise, turned to her grandmother for an explanation, but the old lady had disappeared. "Where did you see them?" she asked.

"Your grandmother showed me a dozen or so and I've come to make an offer."

Her breath caught. "I'm not sure what you mean."

"I'd like for you to have a showing in my gallery in New York. It could mean an immense professional break for you."

Brooke stared at him in surprise. "I'm very grateful, Mr. Reed, but I'm not sure what to say."

"Say yes."

Her heart tripped at the possibilities. "It would be wonderful."

"There is one condition, however," he said, jabbing at the olive in his martini. "I need at least twenty paintings and must have everything in hand by the first of March."

Her heartbeat seemed to stall. "But I'm afraid that's not possible. I have two jobs to work around. I need more time."

"Quit the jobs," he said with a shrug. "This is more important to your future."

Brooke went numb. "I can't."

He gave her a fatherly pat on the shoulder. "No need to make a decision tonight. Think about it a while and let me know."

After the guests had left, Brooke, her stomach in a knot, approached her grandmother. "Tell me the truth, Grandmama, did you engineer this?"

The old lady looked slighted offended. "Dear, this man does not show mediocre artists."

She gave her a sidelong look of skepticism. "Perhaps not, but . . ." She knew it was futile to finish. Grandmama had her ways and would never admit to them. Her logic was almost childlike. If one wanted something, one devised clever ways to get it. She wanted Brooke at home—for good. It was that simple. Yet, she realized, painfully, that the opportunity, however devised, was one at which most artists would jump. How much longer would it be before she got a chance like this? Would she ever?

She kissed her grandmother on the cheek. "You're quite cunning, you know."

The old lady responded with a mysterious smile, then kissed her good night.

When Brooke arrived back in Choctaw Hollow, Butter Creek was oozing over its banks and the weather service was predicting more rain. The prediction came true.

The rain poured in sheets past the windows of the cabin, leaving her even more on edge. Throughout the trip, she'd struggled over the gallery offer until she was exhausted. To let it go was to let go of everything, that all-important promise she'd made to herself. And how could she be sure that her grandmother hadn't influenced the man with some money?

Despite the rain and her inner turmoil, there was something oddly comforting about coming back to the mountains. Seeing Choctaw Hollow from a fresh perspective, she realized she was starting to appreciate its subtle charms. And then, there was Drew.

She lay in bed that night perusing the frustrating maze her life had become when she heard a crack outside the window. She jumped up, but she could see nothing in the rain and darkness. The noise was soon followed by a whoosh, then a crash that sent vibrations rippling across the floor of the cabin. Her heart pounding, she threw on her rain slicker and darted outside, the earth making sucking sounds under her feet. She found the ancient old oak lying across the road leading to the cabin. Her heart sank. She stared at it in dismay for a few moments before she realized that she wouldn't be able to get out except on foot.

Unable to sleep, she sat up the rest of the night reading and sketching to bring calm to the little storm that raged within her. Prolonging her relationship with Drew would only lead to more hurt in the end. The falling tree was another in a multiplying list of frustrations. Yet despite the hardships and her relationship with Drew, she couldn't leave if the best gallery in the world beckoned. She'd made a vow and she intended to keep it.

When dawn finally broke, she threw on jeans, hiking boots, a denim shirt, and a yellow cable-knit sweater and went out to examine the tree. There was a jagged tear at the base of the trunk where it had separated from the roots. All around were puddles of water. She was indeed trapped. There was no way out by car.

She had started back to the cabin to notify the authorities of the mishap when the familiar dark blue Jeep appeared at the end of the road. Her blood surged. She watched as Drew parked in front of the fallen tree and jogged toward her, his hair falling over his forehead. "Need a ride to school?" he asked, his cheeks tinged pink with exertion.

She was momentarily speechless with surprise. "How did you know?"

"A passing motorist reported it and the sheriff's office notified me. Knowing I sometimes need to make house calls, they keep me up on negative road conditions."

He paused and studied her for a moment. "You did come back from the city after all."

"Disappointed?" she asked wryly. Her heart raced at the nearness of him.

A faint smile played on his lips, as he continued to peruse her from her damp, windblown hair to her muddy boots. "Not terribly," he said.

"I'll tell you all about it later, if you can wait."

"Come to Chez Griffin tonight after hours. We can talk about it over dinner."

During the drive to town, Brooke could see the damage wrought by four additional days of rain. As the Jeep crossed the Butter Creek bridge, she could see that areas that had been grass and underbrush were now under water. The creek rolled swiftly downstream, taking with it fallen limbs and other debris.

"The story is that Butter Creek got its name from being so smooth and placid," Drew said. "But every thirty or forty years it seems to go on a rampage. The old-timers say that it has swept houses off their foundations."

"What are the chances of it getting close to the cabin?" she asked.

Drew's face took on a worried look. "If it doesn't stop raining, the chances are excellent," he said, glancing at her briefly as he drove. "Keep a close watch on it."

Brooke tensed, but before she could respond, he stopped in front of the elementary school door. "Keep a very good watch," he added, "hour by hour."

The rain had dwindled to a drizzle by the time Brooke arrived at the clinic later that day. Drew was tending to his last patient, a six-year-old boy with both asthma and flu symptoms. The poor child looked so miserable that Brooke quickly sketched a cartoon of him examining the doctor. It brought a smile to his face.

"Thanks again," Drew said after the boy and his mother left. "You'll make a partner one day yet." Then his smile faded as if he'd been suddenly reminded of something unpleasant.

Brooke swallowed hard. She only wanted to live for now because she knew the future would take her away from him.

Drew removed his lab coat and draped it over a chair. She noticed that his lids were heavy and his broad shoulders drooped with fatigue. "This is the time of the year that I really need help. Sometimes, it seems as though everyone in Choctaw Hollow comes through these doors. But," he added, his expression brightening, "this day is over and the evening is ours, that is, if there's not an emergency.

"Go in and make yourself comfortable. For the 'welcome back' dinner I promised you, Gertie has made us some chicken and dumplings and peach cobbler. I'll run over to the café and get it."

Brooke found Drew's apartment uncharacteristically neat. The medical books that were usually strewn about were in orderly stacks. The little dining room table gleamed. On it was a vase of fresh pink carnations. When had he found the time to buy them? The gesture brought a little tug to her heart.

Ten minutes passed before he returned. In the meantime, Brooke busied herself setting the table with the odd mélange of dishes and flatware that equaled her own.

"Sorry," he said, hurrying through the door. "I had to say hello to everyone. That's life in the small town."

As they sat down to eat, he gave her a lingering look. "Tell me about life in the city."

She wanted to tell him instead how good it was to be with him, but she told him about Grandmama, who, despite her heart "ailment," had given her a spare-no-expense reception, complete with chamber orchestra.

The Biggest Heart in Choctaw Hollow 141

Drew's eyes narrowed in what she took to be disapproval.

Then, cautiously, she told him about the art dealer and his proposal.

There was a beat of silence. "Having your own exhibit in New York is what you've always wanted, isn't it?" he asked finally.

She laid down her fork. "Yes, but I'm not leaving here." Her voice had an edge of determination.

His gaze sharpened. "Perhaps you should think about this some more."

Her blood chilled. "I've made up my mind. I came here with a certain goal in mind and I'm not wavering from it. Besides, you just said you need a lot of help during the winter."

He stroked his jaw and studied her closely. "Forget about me. I can find someone else. If you're looking for encouragement to stay, I'm afraid I can't give it to you. Your future lies somewhere else."

Her mouth went suddenly dry. "You don't understand," she argued, her voice tight.

His brows furrowed. "I understand that people have dreams and that those dreams usually don't include Choctaw Hollow."

She drew a sharp breath. "I have dreams, Drew, and I'll follow them even if I have to detour around the moon," she said hotly. "But in the meantime, I have to remain true to myself. No one can change that, not Grandmama, who has probably engineered this show to lure me back home, and not you."

She jumped up and faced him squarely, her cheeks flaming. "Don't assume, Drew Griffin, that I'm so spoiled that I can be distracted so easily. I'm here for the children of Choctaw Hollow. I don't walk out on my obligations. How dare you suggest that I would?''

She strode across the floor, her footsteps heavy. But he strode after her and caught her elbow, spinning her toward him. His eyes were dark and stormy.

"I'm only suggesting that you think very carefully about what you're doing," he said, his voice low. "You're here on a personal journey and that road has led to a new turn, one unanticipated. Just be sure you know where you're going. You may consider the children in your decision, but you have no obligation toward the clinic." His grip on her arm loosened. "Or me," he added, his voice tight. Strain was apparent on his face even in the dimly lighted room.

A lump formed in her throat. "I know what I want," she countered, pulling away from him. Her defiant gaze swept over his stubbornly set jaw and settled for a brief but burning moment on his eyes. They glinted with intensity.

"Thank you for dinner, Drew," she said, grabbing her coat. "Good night."

Later, at the cabin, as the rain spattered against the windows, Brooke sat numbly in front of the fire, watching the orange flames dance over the logs. Drew's words echoed in her head. She didn't belong here, he'd said. Her destiny was elsewhere. He was telling her to go, to seek out the world away from Choctaw Hollow and away from him. He was as dispassionate about it as if she were a stranger, as if the kisses they'd shared meant nothing.

Despite her attempts to keep them back, hot tears spilled down her cheeks. They came from the crushing realization that there was yet another reason why leaving Choctaw Hollow would never be easy, whether now or later. She was in love with Drew.

When Brooke awoke early Sunday morning after a fitful and sheet-twisting sleep, she discovered in horror that the cabin was surrounded by water. She threw on her clothes and put on a pair of knee-high rubber boots and her slicker. She went outside and stepped off the porch to find the foundation was about three inches under water. She looked dismally toward Butter Creek to find it almost lost in a vast lake. It was marked only by the trees that grew up along its banks. Their bare, twisted branches reached up to a pewter sky from which the rain still fell. The drops came in a dense, beating rhythm that seemed to have an eternal coda.

Her heartbeat quickening, she ran inside the cabin, put all her paintings and sketches inside a portfolio case and stuck it on a high shelf in the kitchen. She locked the cabin and got into the car to move it to higher ground. To her relief, the engine started with a sputter.

Instead of turning toward town, she followed the dirt road that linked her cabin to the Johnicos' house. Jessie would know where to go and what to do. She found the house sitting in water up to the first porch step. Jessie's pickup truck was parked nearby.

Brooke left the car up on the elevated road, waded to the house and knocked on the door, but there was no answer. She knocked louder, but the only response was a light rumble of thunder. Concerned, she decided to check behind the house, when she heard a faint call from the distance. She heard it again, this time a little louder.

"Thaney!"

Brooke recognized Jessie's voice. It was tinged with desperation. Then, Jessie appeared through a clearing. Brooke waved and waded toward her as fast as she could.

Jessie, outfitted in a green rain poncho, was soaked from the hips down. Despite the hood she wore, her face glistened with rain and her dark eyes held fear. "I can't find Thaney," she said breathlessly.

Brooke turned cold. "How long has he been missing?"

"About a half hour." She touched a trembling hand to her forehead. "When he got up this morning, Dog was missing. Before I knew it, Thaney was gone. Now there's no sign of either one of them. I've yelled until I'm hoarse. I'm scared to death. I'm going in to call the sheriff."

Brooke touched her. "Don't worry, we'll find him. "I'll go look while you call. Do you have a rope by chance?" she asked, remembering her water safety training.

"In the shed," she said, pointing next to the house.

Inside, Brooke found a length of rope coiled on a hook. She threw it over her shoulder and as she walked toward the raging stream, a knot formed in her stomach. What chance would a little boy have against such a strong current?

She waded, calling his name, unsure where to look,

but her calls went unanswered. Then she remembered the small pedestrian bridge just downstream toward the cabin. She trudged toward it, the water inching up higher toward the tops of her boots. The rain lashed at her face, leaving her cold and numb.

The bridge would have given both boy and dog access to higher ground, she figured. But when she got to the site of the bridge, she blinked in disbelief. It was gone, swept away in the current.

"Thaney!" she yelled in a mixture of desperation and futility.

"I'm here!" a child's voice answered.

Brooke's heart leaped. Her gaze swept over the surrounding treetops, but she saw nothing. Could she be so desperate to hear his voice that she was imagining it? "I can't see you!" she cried. "Where are you?"

"In the tree where the bridge was." The child's voice was shrill with urgency.

Brooke raised her gaze to find the boy clinging to a young tree not much taller than a man. Water swirled around the trunk inches below the boy's feet.

"I see you," she said. "Hold on tight. Your grandmother has called for help."

But she knew she couldn't leave him for fear the water would sweep him away. And she didn't know if the water level would hold until rescuers found them. She was going to have to try to get him down herself. Trembling, she removed her coat, hat, and boots. She was quickly soaked to the skin, the rain working its icy fingers over her.

She waded toward him until she was waist deep in water. He was yet another twenty feet from her. "I'm going to try to throw this so you can reach it. But don't let go of the tree. Do you hear?"

"Yes," he answered, his eyes wide with fear.

Brooke's heart raced. "All right," she called. "Get ready!" Treading deeper into the water, she took a length of coiled rope and threw it with all her strength but it fell a few feet short of the tree. Her heart sank. She pulled it back, the rope burning her hands as she worked. Now even wetter, the rope was heavier and even harder to pitch.

She threw it again, but it fell even shorter of her target. Reeling it back in, she walked further out, this time almost to her armpits.

"Hurry, Miss Adler," he cried. "My arms hurt."

Fueled by fear and adrenaline, Brooke threw the rope with all the power and concentration she had. The end of it caught just over the branch on which the child was sitting.

She weakened with relief. "Tie the rope around the trunk of the tree," she shouted. She struggled for balance as the water swirled about her.

Clinging to the trunk, the boy rose. But as he reached for the rope on the branch overhead, his foot slipped. Brooke's heart seemed to leap out of her chest as he struggled for balance. He glanced at her, his face pale with fear and relief. "You're doing fine, Thaney," she yelled. "Tie a slip knot like you learned in Scouts."

Thaney worked diligently as Brooke's heart hammered inside her chest. Was she asking too much of such a small boy?

"I got it!" he yelled.

The Biggest Heart in Choctaw Hollow 147

"Stay there for a moment and I'll come after you," she said, her teeth chattering from cold and fear. Taking the other end of the rope, she swam back to the other side of the creek and tied the rope to the closest thing the rope would reach, a tree that was not much more than a sapling. She prayed that it would hold.

Using the rope as a lifeline, she threaded her way across the creek, her breath coming in gasps. The short distance seemed miles. When she got to the tree, she coached the boy to lower himself into her arms. With his feet in the water and his clinging to the limb with his arms, she grabbed him around the waist and held him tightly.

Wobbly with relief, she instructed him to hold on to the rope as they paddled toward the other side. She could feel his small body shivering with fear and cold. "It's all right," she said, treading the murky water. "Just hold on tight."

They were within feet of the opposite bank when a sudden surge of water swept the boy out of her arms. With a scream, he bobbed up in the current, then down. Brooke, her heart thundering in her ears, managed with a desperate, snapping reach to grab the back of his sweatshirt. Suddenly, she felt a sharp, jabbing pain in her back. A fallen limb skirted past the edge of her vision. Ignoring the searing sensation that followed, she towed the gasping child back to the lifeline.

Then, after what seemed to be an eternity, she could feel the ground under her feet. Yet her knees were shaking so that she could hardly support her own weight and the boy's.

"We're safe now," she said, her voice sounding

weak. She carried him a few more yards until she could safely put him down. The water came up to her knees, but past his waist. Weak with relief, it didn't matter at all that her slicker and boots had long since been swept away, that she was so cold that her teeth chattered or that the skin on her back burned. They were safe.

For a moment, she stood still, clinging fast to the little boy.

Suddenly, he started to sob. "Dog," he cried. "I never did find Dog."

An ache spread through her. "Don't give up," she said, trying not to reveal her own fear. "Dogs can often find their way home."

Suddenly, she heard the sound of a motor. A small boat carrying two men appeared in the distance. Her heart surging, she waved wildly in their direction. The boat was quickly upon them and the motor was switched off. The slickers the men wore bore the emblems of the sheriff's office.

"Are you folks all right?" one of them asked.

Brooke nodded. "We're sure happy to see you."

"There are some people up the road who are going to be awful glad to see you," the younger man said.

"Did you find a big black and white dog?" Thaney asked after they were pulled into the boat and outfitted with life jackets.

"No, son," the older man said.

Brooke pulled him closer to her as his bottom lip quivered. Suddenly, she felt exhausted. Soaking wet and shivering from head to toe, she became aware of the increasing pain in her back.

The Johnicos' little house appeared beyond a turn. Brooke was shocked to see that the water was now up to the second porch step. Nearby, Jessie's hands went to her face in a gesture of relief.

Thaney!'' she cried, as an officer lifted him out of the boat and carried him to his grandmother.

Brooke smiled at the tearful reunion as she scrambled out of the boat with the help of the other officer.

"Miss Adler got me down out of a tree," Thaney explained, adding several minutes of dramatic detail, some exaggerated.

Jessie's eyes widened. "Is that true?"

Brooke shrugged. "More or less."

The woman embraced her. "Oh, how could I ever thank you?"

"There's no need to."

"Oh, I'm so relieved," she said, clinging to her. Somebody saw that yellow coat of yours floating by and we were all scared to death. I had the sheriff's office call Dr. Griffin and he practically demanded that they send for the whole U.S. Navy."

Brooke's heart fluttered. "Where is he now?"

"They're setting up a shelter in the gymnasium for people who've had to evacuate, and he got a call that someone there had gone into premature labor."

"Ma'am," one of the sheriff's officers said, "I think you ought to get your back looked at. You've got blood on the back of your shirt."

Brooke touched her spine in alarm, but could see nothing.

"Oh, dear," Jessie said, taking a quick look.

"You folks need to head for higher ground," the officer said. "They're predicting more rain tonight."

After gathering up a few items from the cabin, including some clothing, her portfolio, easel, and paints, Brooke loaded them into the back of her car and drove toward town, followed by Jessie and Thaney in their pickup truck. With no sign of Drew at the shelter, she drove on to the clinic. It was dark and empty.

She unlocked the door and waited. She changed into dry jeans and a loose shirt, wincing as she pulled away the shirt that had stuck to the wound on her back. Her hair had dried but it was stiff from the muddy creek water. She needed a shower, but hesitated until her back was examined.

But it wasn't the injury that needed attention so much as her heart. In the last few hours, she'd known the most terror of her life, and she'd known the most longing. In those terrifying moments in the water, it was Drew her heart had cried out for, and at this moment she wanted nothing more than the comfort of his embrace.

Suddenly, she heard the key turn in the lock and she raced to the door. Her heart lurched as he entered. His hair was damp, the shoulders of his raincoat beaded with water. Their eyes locked. It took all of Brooke's will not to run to him. But he didn't come to her. Instead, he stood immobile, as if made of stone. His only show of emotion was to close his eyes and to take a deep breath.

"I made it out of the flood, but my coat and boots didn't," she said, making a feeble attempt at humor. "I hope I didn't worry you too much."

The Biggest Heart in Choctaw Hollow

The corner of his mouth twitched almost imperceptibly. "You're remarkable Brooke. You keep proving me wrong. For that, you have my utmost respect."

His words gnawed at her heart. She wanted to hear more, but more was not to come.

"Let's take a look at your back," he said, his tone maddeningly professional.

She nodded, suppressing a lump in her throat. If he cared for her as much as she cared for him, today of all days would have made him show it. But he didn't, she saw with dismay. She was in love with a man who didn't love her.

Chapter Ten

Brooke, her throat raw with emotion, sat quietly as Drew treated her back. Besides the sting of having the scrape cleaned, she was filled with a deeper ache. She couldn't understand why he'd distanced himself from her when she needed his comfort the most.

"You have some fairly deep bruises and abrasions and you'll experience soreness for a few days," he said almost tonelessly. "The tetanus shot I gave you shouldn't cause any reaction."

He placed a loose bandage over the wound and re-tied her examination gown at the neck. His fingers lingered for a moment, causing her blood to stir. Then he turned toward her, his eyes murky.

"Perhaps you're not so much out of your element after all." He gave her a slight smile with a trace of sadness to it. "You're a paradox, Brooke, and an interesting one at that. You'll be remembered here long after you're gone."

"Even by you?" she asked with a cheerfulness she didn't feel.

His lips tightened in a grim line, but he offered no reply.

Brooke scooted off the table. "I'm touched," she said, bristling. "I didn't realize you cared."

He grabbed her by the shoulders and forced her to face him. His blue-gray gaze burned into hers. "Of course I care. I care about all my patients. I care about everyone in this town and that includes you."

Brooke's cheeks tingled with color. He might as well have said nothing.

"I want you to stay here tonight," he said after a brief silence. "I'll get Jessie and Thaney to stay with you. I'll spend the night at the shelter."

She shook her head in protest. "I can manage at the shelter like everyone else."

His chin crinkled stubbornly. "Stay here," he repeated sternly. "I can be of some use at the shelter. You can take my bed and Jessie and Thaney can sleep on the cots."

Before she could refuse, he thrust the keys to his apartment in her hand. "You've had a hard day. Get some rest. You deserve it. I'll have food sent over from the café."

Brooke stood at the window as he disappeared into the rain. Illuminated by the street lights, it fell in a steady, golden patter. It also fell in her heart.

Replaying the rigors of the day, she waited until she

saw the lights of Jessie's truck cut through the darkness. She held open the clinic door.

Jessie threw back the hood of her flowing, green rain poncho. "How are you feeling?" she asked, her voice ringing with sympathy. "We got here just as quick as we could."

"I'm really fine," she said as Thaney put his arms around her hips. She knelt down and hugged the boy. "How's the little artist?"

"I'm fine, but you know what?" he asked, his eyes round and sad. "We never did find Dog."

A little ache coursed through her. "I'm so sorry," she said, stroking his shiny black hair.

As she rose, Jessie's eyes met hers in a knowing look. "The creek keeps rising," she said, her voice full of worry. "The last report was that some of the houses and cabins along Butter Creek may be swept away if it doesn't stop soon. Some of the trailers up by the river are already gone."

Brooke felt a jab of sorrow and fear, not for herself but for Jessie and the others. She glanced dismally out the window. "All we can do is hope for the best."

Jessie nodded. "What matters most is that we're safe. I can't tell you how grateful I am. I'll just never be able to repay you."

Before Brooke could reply, there was a knock on the door. She opened it to find a towering teenage boy holding a large bag. "It's your dinner, ma'am, from the Green Tomato."

She gave him a generous tip. "How is your family holding up during all this rain?"

The Biggest Heart in Choctaw Hollow 155

"They're at the shelter, ma'am. We live along the creek."

They sat down to a dinner of meat loaf, scalloped potatoes, green beans, and corn. With it came homemade rolls and apple cobbler. Thaney ate heartily, but Brooke, despite the day's ordeal, had little appetite.

"My husband built our little yellow house," Jessie said, her eyes alight with nostalgia. "Finished it just before Thaney's mother was born. It wasn't much, but it was our castle."

As Jessie told of the people who lived along the creek, Thaney nodded to sleep over his plate. His grandmother carried him to bed.

Brooke's heart went out to the Johnicos and the others and she began to realize her growing fondness and admiration for the people of Choctaw Hollow. There was no pretension, none of the curt treatment that city people often gave strangers. Despite their hardships, their optimism remained.

Brooke was peering out the kitchen window into the wet night when Jessie returned.

"My Grandmother used to say that all that's good comes from the sky," the older woman said. "Even the winds and the rains, she said, have good hidden inside them."

Brooke turned to her with a little smile. "That's something to think about, especially tonight."

Jessie nodded grimly, then set about tidying up the kitchen in the absent manner of someone troubled. She watered a drooping plant, then set about rearranging the refrigerator, tossing out a wilted and faded stalk of celery and a moldy jar of leftover soup. "Isn't this just like a man?'' she asked, producing a shriveled apple. "Bless his heart. I hope he gets some sleep tonight, but I know good and well he won't."

She tossed out a half-eaten candy bar. "This refrigerator tells you something about his priorities. Work, work, work. After Cheryl, he just made his work his life. It was like it was his way of forgetting."

Brooke's heart took a little leap. "What happened with Cheryl?" Her voice came out stiff.

Jessie emptied a large jar containing a single olive then leaned against the sink. "They were to be married after he finished his residency. He even talked to me about making the cake. But she decided suddenly that she couldn't take living in Choctaw Hollow again. She'd become a city girl and she was in a hurry to make her fortune in real estate. Waiting four years until Drew finished his obligation here would cost her money. So just like that," she said with a snap of her fingers, "Cheryl was gone. That was two years ago. Now, she's a big real estate success story. My cousin saw her picture in the paper. She was standing in front of her own office building. And for money and recognition, she gave up one of the best men alive." The corner of Jessie's mouth quirked in consternation. "Growing up poor had an effect on her to be sure, but I never thought it would make her shun her roots and the people who cared about her. As for Drew, he took it hard but he did his best not to show it. He just worked harder and longer."

Brooke, her eyes riveted on Jessie, bit her bottom lip.

"To tell the truth," the older woman continued,

The Biggest Heart in Choctaw Hollow 157

"Cheryl did him a favor, but a man doesn't get over that sort of thing easily."

Jessie's words haunted Brooke as she tossed sleeplessly that night in Drew's bed. There was a wall around his heart that seemed impenetrable. All hope seemed to vanish as she played back all the scenes of their relationship. He'd been wary of her background and of her commitment to Choctaw Hollow. He'd warned her that nothing could come of their relationship. But worst of all, in that moment they met after she and Thaney were thought to be in peril or worse, he'd offered no arms to hold her. Would he never care for anyone again the way he cared for Cheryl?

Her eyes filling with tears, Brooke could stand his bed no longer. The pillow held faint traces of his scent. The mattress had borne the imprint of his body. She rose and tore off the top layer of blankets. Out of one, she made a pallet on top of a braided rug at the side of the bed. She fashioned a pillow out of another. She covered herself with a spare quilt and struggled to find escape in sleep.

She knew what it was to be hurt in love and she understood Drew's hesitancy to avoid such pain again. But for her, she thought darkly, it was too late.

When Brooke awoke the next day, Drew was standing over her with his arms folded across his chest.

She sat up with a start and rubbed her eyes. "What are you doing here?"

He smiled wryly. "I live here, Merry Sunshine. It was the logical place for me to come to take a shower and change clothes. Fortunately, you slept through the entire procedure."

"You could have waited, you know." She avoided his eyes for fear she would lose herself in them.

He looked at his watch. "I did, but noon was my limit."

She leaned forward. "It's that late?"

"It's later. It's one-thirty."

She gasped. "How could I have slept through half the day?"

"How could you sleep on the floor?" he shot back. "Suppose you tell me why."

She pulled the covers around her neck. "I just wanted to, that's all," she said defensively.

He cocked a skeptical eyebrow. "It's not good for your back."

"My back doesn't matter. What about the creek?"

A muscle twitched in his jaw. "First, your back does matter and second, the creek is still rising. The houses along the creek are standing in one to two feet of water, including the cabin. The ones on lower ground are up to their windows in water. Some may no longer be habitable."

Her heart sank as she thought of the families who had so little to begin with.

"At least," he added, his gaze piercing, "no lives were lost, thanks, in part, to you. It wasn't a bad feat for someone who couldn't make the school swim team." There was an almost imperceptible touch of pride in his eyes.

Brooke felt a tinge of color rise to her cheeks. "Anyone would have done what I did."

The Biggest Heart in Choctaw Hollow 159

"That's what I told the reporters you'd probably say."

Brooke's spine straightened, bringing a shot of pain. "Reporters?"

"They're covering the flood for the city newspaper and television stations. I told them you were resting. I hope you don't mind."

Brooke shook her head. "Being an Adler is enough. I don't need any more notoriety."

"It may be a little late for that. Thaney has told them all about it, although I suspect some of the details have been rather lavishly embroidered."

She gasped. "What do you mean?"

Amusement played in his eyes. "Can you throw a wet rope a mile?"

She clamped her hands over her temples and shook her head. "What else?"

"There may have been a shark circling nearby as well." The corner of his mouth lifted in a crooked smile.

Brooke groaned. "Please, no more."

"Don't worry," he said, sitting at the edge of the pallet, "that's all, at least as far as Thaney is concerned. But there's another development. Your grandmother is hysterical. Getting no answer at the cabin, of course, she called the sheriff's office and ultimately they placed her in contact with me. She wants you to call her right away. In addition, she's sending the chauffeur after you tomorrow morning."

Brooke scrambled to her feet. "She can't do that," she retorted, pacing about the floor. Her rosebud print

Victorian nightgown swirled about her bare feet. "I'm not going."

Drew took her by the shoulders. "It won't hurt you to rest up for a few days. The schools are closed and the cabin is uninhabitable for the time being."

"But you'll need me at the clinic," she protested.

"Jessie will help."

Brooke wrenched herself away from him. "Admit it. You don't want me here, do you? You've been trying to get me to go home ever since I came."

His jaw hardened. "What does it matter whether or not I want you to stay? You're leaving in the spring, aren't you?"

A knot formed in her stomach. The question needed no answer. After that, her work would be finished.

"Cheer up," he said, his voice tight. "The sky is supposed to clear tomorrow and they're predicting a change in the weather pattern. We'll all feel better after this downpour stops. And one more thing," he said. "Thaney has a surprise for you."

He took a few strides toward the door, then turned. "I'll see you before you leave."

With a click of the door, he was gone.

She fought back tears. When were people going to stop thinking that they knew better than she what was best for her?

She dressed quickly in jeans, a blue plaid flannel shirt, and a red cotton cardigan and went into the kitchen, where she found a note from Jessie along with a plate of club sandwiches. "Thaney will be running in and out. If he bothers you, send him to the clinic."

She fortified herself with a sandwich and a glass of milk before calling her grandmother.

"My precious darling!" the old woman exclaimed. "I have never been so proud and so terrified. How could you not call your Grandmama and have her worry about you so?"

"Grandmama, I intended—"

"Dr. Halpern had to be summoned," she interrupted. "I was simply beside myself."

"I'm very sorry," she said, "but please, Grandmama, there's no reason to send Ned down."

"He's already on his way, dear," she responded. "He's going to spend the night somewhere on the road and be there first thing in the morning. You must come home. You have nowhere to live now. Trust Grandmama. I'll see you tomorrow."

Brook slapped down the receiver in exasperation. She was staring at the phone, trying to sort out the chaos within and without when the door burst open. In came a glowing Thaney. At his side was Dog.

Brooke jumped to her feet. "Where did you find him?" She ran over and put her arms around the dog's neck.

"Somebody found him and brought him to the sheriff," he said. "He couldn't get back home because of the water."

She hugged the boy. "This is wonderful."

"I drew a picture," he said. "I'll show you."

The child skipped off into the dining area and pulled a sketch pad from a shelf. Proudly, he presented a crayoned picture of dog being transported over the water by an angel.

Her heart swelled. "Thaney, it's just terrific."

She studied the details closely. Dog's markings were rendered faithfully. The angel's wings were accurately shaped and spread against a gray sky. Little waves bobbed on the water. In the background were houses half-submerged. Suddenly, an idea came to her as clearly as if it had been ringed by flashing lights. This drawing and others could be used as covers on greeting cards. The cards could be sold to raise funds to help flood victims.

She presented the idea to the boy and his eyes widened. "Would the picture have my name on it?"

"Absolutely," she said, giving him another hug.

The next morning, she waited for the inevitable. Shortly after ten, it arrived. Ned, driving the old but brightly polished black Mercedes, parked in front of the clinic. She didn't want to leave, but her heart leaped at the sight of the kindly butler. He'd barely gotten out of the car when her arms were already around his neck.

"How good it is to see you, Missy. We're real proud of you, we are."

"Oh, Ned," she said, almost wishing she'd hadn't finally answered the calls from reporters the night before. "You shouldn't even mention it."

His eyes caught just over her shoulder. Brooke turned to find Drew standing just outside the clinic door. His eyes locked on hers and a little spear seemed to shoot through her heart.

She introduced the two men and they shook hands.

"Have a safe trip," Drew said, his voice tight. He

The Biggest Heart in Choctaw Hollow 163

came forward, as if to take her in his arms, but he stopped in mid stride and simply took her hand in his for a moment. Her heart leaped, then fell as he released his fingers. Silently, she got into the car. As they drove away, she turned to watch his form grow smaller, until he faded out of sight.

She tried to obscure the ache in her heart in a rattle of small talk. She told of Choctaw Hollow, the children and their drawings.

"If I may be so bold as to inquire," he said, taking the car around a sharp curve, "you haven't had much to say about the young man."

She swallowed hard, then tried to explain in even tones Drew's mission in the town. "Other than that, I don't know what to say," she said obliquely.

Ned, appearing unconvinced that that was the end of the story, scratched his iron gray hair but said nothing.

"Don't tell Grandmama, but I have a second job—working in his clinic," Brook offered.

"You know you can trust me, Missy," he said, glancing at her with a smile. "We've always had our little secrets, haven't we? Remember the time you asked me to teach you to play poker? Your grandmother would have certainly disapproved."

Brooke smiled. Then, slowly, she confessed that she'd concealed the fact she'd been in an accident and that in the beginning, she was having trouble making ends meet. "She would hire kidnappers to remove me from the mountains if she knew."

"Indeed, she would." Silence, broken only by the soft hum of the engine, followed.

"Missy," he said gravely, "I don't want you to fret, but I think there's something you should know."

With a pang of alarm, she turned toward him. "What is it?"

"The paycheck I got from your grandmother yesterday bounced."

Brooke's stomach snapped into a knot. "I don't understand."

"Neither do I, Missy. I'm not sure how to tell her."

Numbed, Brooke stared through the windshield. "There's always been plenty of money for everything, no matter how reckless Grandmama's spending has been. Grandfather always saw to that. He spoiled her terribly."

Then the significance of her words bore down on her like a weight. Could Grandmama's spending finally have caught up with her? Brooke shook her head. Impossible. If the checking account were empty, there were others. There had always been money somewhere—a dividend check from some long-forgotten stock, a royalty payment, a rental payment. Money came in the mail every day.

"It could have been the garden party," he suggested. "Hannah said the catering bill alone was eight thousand dollars. There were ice sculptures, foie gras from France, and caviar from Russia. Then she bought some things for the house, an armoire and an Oriental rug."

"But that's typical for Grandmama," Brooke said. "Please don't worry." But during the long miles home, she wasn't able to heed her own advice.

* * *

When Ned pulled into the circular drive in front of the old mansion, Brooke felt more separated from her past than ever before. Her experiences at Choctaw Hollow had changed her and nothing at home would be the same again.

Despite her alienation from the society world in which she was brought up, Drew, she thought ruefully, continued to see her as part of it. And now she understood the roots and the depth of his feelings. He'd lost Cheryl to the quest for wealth and status. But she was not Cheryl. She was not even a typical Adler. The irony of it was bitter. Once men were interested in her because of her background. Now, that background was keeping Drew at a distance.

Grandmama appeared in the doorway with Hannah in the background. There were hugs all around.

"Now, look at you," Grandmama said, frowning at Brooke's jeans and hiking boots. "Such clothing. Be glad that you're in my extra good graces or I'd make you change."

"Can you suggest a frock for a flood?" Brooke asked, tongue in cheek.

The old lady gave her a censuring look. "Now, now. Let's have some tea. I want to hear about everything, including plans for the exhibit."

"There's not going to be an exhibit, Grandmama," Brooke said gently.

The old lady set her cup in her saucer with a clatter. "I don't understand. It's the opportunity you've always wanted."

"I have my obligations in Choctaw Hollow and I intend to live up to them."

She turned pale. She set down her cup and saucer and placed a hand over her chest. "You are serious about this, aren't you, Brooke?"

"Yes, Grandmama, I am."

The old woman took a deep breath, but said nothing.

Brooke sat beside her on the deeply padded sofa and placed an arm around her shoulder. "I'm afraid we have something even more important to talk about."

The next morning, as Grandmama fanned herself with a linen and lace handkerchief, an audit was ordered of the old woman's finances. Two days later, the family accountant, a white-haired, slightly stooped contemporary of Brooke's grandfather, asked to speak to Brooke privately in his downtown office.

His expression was pinched. "At this moment, your grandmother is living like a rich woman on a middle-class income."

Her nerves jumped in surprise. "How can that be?"

"Ingrid, rather your grandmother, appears to have gotten some poor investment advice in the last year. To make a long story short, the family fortune is no longer a fortune."

Chapter Eleven

Stunned, Brooke stared at him in disbelief. But the anxiety surging through her was not for herself, but her grandmother. "How bad is it?" she finally managed to ask.

"Your grandmother is seventy-two years old. If she lives an extraordinarily long life, there's not a lot of time left for the stock market to work in her favor and recoup her losses. But there are some things we can do."

"Like what?" Her voice had a choking quality to it. How could Grandmama bear up to such news?

He tapped his fingers on his desk. "I figure if we can sell the commercial property, she'll be able to maintain a reasonable standard of living for the rest of her life. She can even keep the maid and the butler, providing she cuts down on the parties. The problem is that the commercial property and the income it brings make up the entirety of your trust fund."

Her heart kicked. She'd looked forward to earning the right to turn it over to charity. Yet she had to be certain that Grandmama was properly cared for. And Ned and Hannah, who had been surrogate parents to her, couldn't be let go. She took a deep breath. "Take it," she said. "Do with it whatever you must."

He studied her for a moment. "Are you sure? You realize that the only thing you will likely inherit now is the house, and of course that might have to be sold if your grandmother gets into serious trouble again."

She swallowed hard. "I understand."

"All right, then," he said, closing the file. "I'll get with the attorney and we'll start on this right away."

"There's something else," she said. "Perhaps you could shield her from at least part of the truth. I don't want her to know that she's leaving me with almost nothing. I never wanted anything, but she has never been able to understand that. I'm afraid the complete truth would be too much for her."

He smiled gently. "I'll do my best."

"And another thing," she said. "She obviously needs help managing money. Please help me keep her out of trouble."

"I care very much for Ingrid, you know," he said. "I would be pleased to do it."

Brooke left the building waiting for the sense of relief that she thought would come when she was free of the trust fund. But she felt very little, hardly even the biting December wind on her face. Grandmama was in trouble, she was in love with a man who didn't

The Biggest Heart in Choctaw Hollow 169

love her, and her own future was frighteningly uncertain. She had sought to simplify her life and never had it seemed so complicated.

When Brooke arrived in Choctaw Hollow, the sun shone almost mockingly. Suddenly, she was grateful for the work that awaited her. It would blunt the turmoil that raged inside her. There were drawings to select for the cards that would be printed to benefit victims of the flood. In the city, she'd found a printer. Now all she needed was a small bank loan to pay for them. Once printed, there would be marketing and distribution to worry about and it all had to be done as quickly as possible.

Much of Choctaw Hollow seemed hung out to dry. Furniture sat on lawns and porches. Curtains and quilts hung from clotheslines. Mud and silt were being hosed from sidewalks and driveways. When she got to the cabin, she was surprised to find the windows and front door open. Thaney and Dog stood on the porch.

Brooke parked the car, got out, and pulled Thaney into her arms "What's going on?"

Before he could answer, Jessie appeared in the doorway. "Welcome back. We got the cabin all cleaned up and dried out for you. Drew got an extra key from Mr. Krauthammer."

Her heart stirred. Stunned, Brooke stepped inside, where a fire was crackling in the hearth and all seemed to be in order. "Jessie, this is so nice of you, but what about your own house?"

"I've gotten plenty of help of my own," she said. "We've had lots of volunteers out here. That's the way things are in Choctaw Hollow. When there's trouble, we all pitch in."

Speechless, Brooke paced across the wooden planks of the cabin floor.

"Fortunately, not much water actually got inside." Jessie said. "The floors are still damp, but it's livable.

"I don't know how to thank you," she said.

"Thank Dr. Griffin." she said. "He swept most of the water out."

Brooke's heart jumped. "He shouldn't have."

"You could be right," Jessie said with a shrug. "The poor man is just worn out. I made him go home and go to bed. The clinic has been a madhouse for the last few days—colds, coughs, asthma attacks. Then old Mr. Madsen's heart flared up because of the flood and one of the Johnson kids stepped on a nail. Mrs. Daugherty slipped on a wet floor and broke her arm. Well, you get the picture."

Brooke nodded as a little twinge passed through her heart.

"Now, you get some rest, too," Jessie said, her tone motherly. "The school is reopening tomorrow."

But after Jessie, Thaney, and Dog had gone home, she found herself unable to rest, unable to draw, and unable to think about anything but Drew. Why would he do this for her when he had so little time?

Instinctively, she sat down and wrote a thank you note. She slipped it into an envelope, along with a quickly drawn cartoon of Drew attacking waves of water with a broom. She got into the car and drove to the clinic, where he would find it under the door when he opened up in the morning.

The Biggest Heart in Choctaw Hollow 171

It was almost dusk when she parked on Main Street. Except for a cluster of cars around the Green Tomato Café, the town was almost deserted. She got out of the car and thrust it under the clinic door. She turned and was several steps away when she heard the door open. Her heart leaped as she turned to find Drew's large frame in the doorway.

"Special delivery?" he asked, holding up the envelope. He wore a rumpled blue scrub suit and a teasing smile.

Her blood raced at the sight of him. "I didn't mean to disturb you. I only wanted to thank you for what you did today."

"I thought I heard someone outside, and when I went to the door, I found this," he said, waving the note. "No apology needed."

"Don't you ever rest?" she asked.

"On occasion. This doesn't happen to be one of them." He held the door open. "Please come in."

She shook her head. "I really should go. There's school tomorrow."

He shrugged. "There will be patients tomorrow, too. Come on. There's hot chocolate on the stove."

Before she could answer, he stepped out on the sidewalk, grabbed her hand, and pulled her inside, past the waiting room and into his apartment. The light from several reading lamps gave it a golden glow. Several books and journals lay on the floor beside a rocking chair.

"Now, what do we have here?" he asked, opening the envelope. "Hate mail, fan mail, a love letter, an eviction notice?"

"You're giddy," she said. "How much sleep have you been getting?"

"More than I got as an intern," he mumbled, reading the note at the same time. He unfolded the cartoon and smiled. It was that lopsided smile that she would always remember no matter where life took her.

She shifted her gaze away from him, in an attempt to ease the pain of their inevitable parting. "I didn't know how else to thank you."

"I'll show you how you can thank me," he said, his eyes sparkling with desire. He drew her into his arms and brushed his lips teasingly against hers while her heart soared wildly in her throat. He brushed back her bangs and kissed her forehead and the tip of her nose. Then his lips settled on hers, warm and possessing. In that moment, she wanted time to stop, to be in his arms forever, to feel the caressing warmth of his lips and the beat of his heart against her breast.

Suddenly, he released her, his breathing heavy and his eyes murky with emotion. "Don't give me any more excuses to kiss you."

Her breath caught in her throat. "What do you mean?"

"A country doctor who hardly knows what fork to use and an heiress—What kind of combination is that? We're from different worlds, Brooke. I seem to keep forgetting that we shouldn't be playing kissing games." There was a tinge of bitterness in his voice.

She stared at him in defiance. "Stop calling me an heiress. At the moment, there are just eight hundred dollars in my bank account, all earned with my own little hands. Furthermore, the accountant has just dis-

The Biggest Heart in Choctaw Hollow 173

covered that Grandmama has squandered a good deal of the family fortune on parties, cruises, and bad investments.''

She took a deep breath to steady herself. ''My trust fund? It will go to support Grandmama for the rest of her life. But it doesn't matter, Drew. Wealth has always brought me more pain than pleasure. I don't need it. I'm made of more than that.''

A muscle twitched in his jaw. ''It's more complicated than that. Don't you see, Brooke? You could be penniless and nothing would change. Your future is elsewhere and you know it.''

Brooke felt a deep chill. It was true. There was no way around it.

He sat on the edge of an armchair, his broad shoulders slumped. His eyes were shadowed, his cheeks covered with a day's growth of beard. Underneath all that raw masculinity was a hint of vulnerability that Brooke had never seen before.

''Remember when we talked about enjoying our time together and not taking things seriously?'' he asked. ''I'm not sure I can do that. I'm not sure you can either.''

''How do you know I can't?'' Her skin prickled with indignity. ''What makes you think that I can't walk away from these mountains and never look back except for the children? What makes you think that I could never leave without taking a piece of you with me? What makes you think that I could fall in love with a man who dislikes what I represent?''

His expression hardened. ''If you're impervious to

all that, why do you melt in my arms like chocolate on a summer day?

Her cheeks burned. "You only wish."

He stood, his mouth twisted in bitter irony. "You're lying, Brooke, and so am I. You're not very good at it. It's not your style and it's not mine. So let's stop this before it goes any farther, before it's too late. Let's keep things strictly professional from now on. It's for your good as much as it is mine."

Her breath stalled in her chest. "I couldn't agree with you more," she finally managed to say. She lifted her chin as if the gesture would restore her pride. Perhaps he hadn't crossed that threshold yet in which his heart would be irretrievably lost. Perhaps he never would. But for her, she thought bitterly, it was too late.

For the next few days, she had the children draw pictures of the flood. At the same time, she did her own painting and sketching. She worked fervently, her style taking on a wild, unfinished, almost desperate edge that had never emerged before. In the hauntingly quiet evenings in the cabin, Drew appeared in every line, in every stroke of the brush.

He wasn't waiting until May to say good-bye to her. He was saying it now. The thought filled her with grief and pain. How could she last five more months in a town that was full of his presence? Well, she would, she resolved grimly. For the children's sake she would.

The waiting room was almost empty when she arrived at the clinic for her end-of-the-week duties. She put on a cheerful face for the waiting patients, but her

The Biggest Heart in Choctaw Hollow   175

heart was heavy as she went about her tasks. She'd contemplated asking Drew to find someone else, but she needed the money to help finance the greeting card project. And then there was the matter of her pride. In quitting, she would reveal the depth of her feelings.

Fifteen minutes passed before she saw him. He opened the door and ushered out old Mr. Weatherbee. One arthritic hand was on his cane, the other on Drew's arm. Their eyes met in one searing second.

"Hello, Brooke," he said stiffly.

"Good afternoon, doctor," she said, then quickly turned her attention to Mr. Weatherbee, her heart racing.

An hour later, the last patient, a teenager recovering from a sprained ankle, was gone, and the clinic was uncharacteristically quiet. Brooke worked on the billing while Drew busied himself in the examination room, seemingly spending an inordinate amount of time rearranging items on shelves and wiping down countertops. As she watched his tall, white-coated form move about, Brooke sensed he was avoiding her. She missed the easy banter, the casual camaraderie, the dialogue—bordering on flirtatious—that they'd shared.

Finally, he appeared in the doorway. "How is your back?" Brooke noted that he still looked tired and pale.

"Much better," she said. "Grandmama insisted that her own doctor come over and look at it."

His lips tightened into a strained smile. "Grandmama doesn't trust country doctors?"

Brooke felt uneasy. "You have to make allowances

for Grandmama. She's never had a life outside her own little milieu. That's what has made her colorfully, wonderfully, yet sadly neurotic. You would hate Grandmama, but not for long. She's almost a caricature of herself and of high society. For having so much, she has been very deprived, deprived of the satisfaction of earning what she has, deprived of having to reach and strain for something. Getting everything handed to you all your life can be a hollow experience. It's an experience that has been repeated often in my family. My mother didn't survive it."

He looked at her intently from under perfect, slightly arched brows. "And that is how you, the dissident debutante, came to be."

"By understanding Grandmama, perhaps you can understand me."

His eyes searched her face; the dimple in his chin deepened in contemplation, but he said nothing.

"To answer your question," she continued, "Dr. Halpern said I'd received excellent care and that he wouldn't have done anything differently. It was Grandmama who asked, not me. I already knew that."

A smile tugged at the corner of his mouth. "When it comes to bodies, it's good to know I have the healing touch." His smile faded. "With hearts and minds, I'm not so sure, my own included."

Brooke thought bitterly of Cheryl and her spirits sank even further. Perhaps Drew would never love her, but had the experience with Cheryl left him unable to love again? Even if he could never love her, she cared too much for him to want him never to love anyone again.

"What's wrong?" he asked. "You look as if you just lost your best friend."

The color in her cheeks deepened. "We're not talking about business, are we?"

He unbuttoned his collar and gave his tie a yank. "I don't suppose we are." He turned his gaze away from her.

"Speaking of business, let me show you what the children have done." Her tone was cool and businesslike but her heart was beating like a thousand drums at his mere presence.

She took her portfolio case from behind her desk and laid it open. One by one, she showed him dozens of brightly colored drawings of the area. She'd instructed the children to show the mountains at their best, to portray the courage and perseverance of the people. In one picture, stick figures stood hand in hand against a background of water which had risen halfway up the mountain. One was simply a painting of one side of Choctaw Hollow's main street with each building in brilliant, surreal colors.

She explained the card project. "I'll get them printed in the city and Grandmama will introduce them at a party—what else? I'll make sure she keeps the expenses low. I thought at the same time, we can have a showing here and play up all the children's work as well. Perhaps we can have a theme and tie it in with Valentine's Day, a sort of mountain valentine."

Drew held up a hand in a cautioning gesture. "Where, may I ask, is the money coming from, since Grandmama's finances are in a state of peril?"

She shot him a look of indignation. "You don't believe the story about the family money?"

"Your grandmother's exaggerations seem to be legend."

"Grandmama doesn't understand how bad it is. I don't want her to know that it's my trust fund that will be supporting her. She would die of humiliation."

Drew cocked his head and studied her for a moment. Her pulse danced in her throat. "Where is the money coming from, then? It's not cheap to have thousands of cards printed."

"I'll get a loan," she said quickly.

He looked at her quizzically. "What are you going to use for collateral?"

"My car," she answered softly.

He stroked an angular jaw. "I think I can help you. I'll talk to old Mr. Weatherbee's son. He runs the bank."

Her spirits lifted. "You would do that?"

"Of course. I care about Choctaw Hollow."

A deep ache pierced her heart. Was he only doing it for Choctaw Hollow?

A brief pause followed. "Brooke, in the beginning I didn't expect you to last more than a few weeks. Now, you've done this. Again, I couldn't have been more wrong about you. I'm sorry."

"No apology is necessary," she said.

She zipped up the portfolio, stood, and wished him a good night. The emotional turmoil raging inside her had left her exhausted.

* * *

The Biggest Heart in Choctaw Hollow 179

Mr. Weatherbee's son was quick to approve the loan. After receiving his call, Brooke took a day off from school and drove the original artwork to the city. The cards, the printer assured, would be ready in plenty of time for Valentine's Day. In the meantime, Grandmama promised to enlist the aid of her charity circle and its publicity committee.

Upon returning to Choctaw Hollow, Brooke again tried to bury her feelings in her work and in her art, but the same dull ache remained. She continued with Thaney's private lessons, marveling at the progress he was making. Nurturing Thaney's considerable talent and seeing to the card project were among her few joys.

When the trial cards arrived at the school for her approval before final printing, Brooke was elated. The colors were beautiful, the art charmingly primitive and childlike. The children were overjoyed. Mr. Krauthammer smiled from ear to ear and even the mayor came by to have a look. Between treating a baby with an ear infection and a child with a broken wrist, Drew studied the cards with quiet pride.

"I'll get Jessie to help me at the clinic for the next few weeks," he said. "You need to be spending your time on this."

Brooke consented almost with relief. She'd begun to approach her work at the clinic with dread, because her heart ached with every beat in which she was in his presence. Although they kept a reasonable distance from each other, she couldn't avoid hearing his voice, and seeing at work the qualities that had endeared him to her.

The cards arrived in stores on the first of February, followed by the arrival of a reporter from the city paper and several television crews. They followed Brooke into the classroom and filmed the children, along with some of the damage still remaining from the flood. Afterwards, sales of the cards soared. Brooke was stunned by the outpouring of support.

During the week before Valentine's Day, Mr. Krauthammer called her into his office.

"We're real pleased with what you've done with the kids here," he said, tapping his finger on a box of cards. "It has not only been good for them, but for the community as a whole. We were wondering if you'd consider staying on in Choctaw Hollow. We've never had a permanent art teacher before, but we think we can manage to find the money for one. You've made a big difference in some of these children's lives."

Brooke was struck speechless. "I'm very grateful," she finally managed to say. "I'd like some time to think it over."

Later, at the cabin, Brooke sat at her easel. Her sketch pad had laid blank in front of her for hours. How could she stay here for another year? It wasn't Choctaw Hollow from which she sought to escape. She needed an escape from the pain in her heart. Staying would only prolong it.

She'd made up her mind to leave until a letter arrived in the mail the next day. It was from a major card company. She read the letter once, then twice, her hands trembling. The company was interested in art by children in impoverished areas. There were roy-

The Biggest Heart in Choctaw Hollow   181

alty possibilities, not just from cards, but from calendars and posters. Scholarship funds could be established from royalties.

In disbelief, she reread the letter. Company representatives would like to come down and discuss matters with her and school officials.

The next few days were a whirl of activity. The school board scrambled to a meeting. Representatives of the card company came. Mr. Krauthammer pleaded with her to stay. After all, scholarships could be at stake. There were plenty of other capable art teachers, she'd told them, but she'd soon let them know of her decision.

When she rose from her seat at the school board meeting, she turned to find Drew standing in the back of the room. His arms were folded across his chest. Her pulse jumped in surprise.

He took her elbow. "I'll walk you to your car."

The February night had a crystalline quality as if the dampness would transform itself into snow at any moment. After being greeted, thanked, and encouraged to stay by everyone passing through the parking lot, Brooke was left alone with Drew.

The lamplight gave his eyes a glittering intensity. "I don't want you to get the wrong idea about why I'm here."

Puzzled, she stared at him. "I'm not sure I understand."

"They can encourage you to stay, but I'm not going to."

Her cheeks, though nearly numb with cold, stung. "You must think that I should go rushing back where

I belong—to charity balls and bridge parties," she said indignantly. "But it doesn't matter what you think, Drew. I'm thoroughly capable of making up my own mind. I'm going to stay and get this project established. I have to help these children even if it means having to live in the same town with you."

His jaw stiffened, but he said nothing as she got into her little car and tearfully sped away, leaving him standing in the freezing mist.

Brooke spent Valentine's Day with a lump in her throat. All week, she'd watched the children draw hearts and cupids. Despite the richness they brought to her life, there was a deep, gnawing ache on the underside of her heart. Standing in a classroom surrounded by symbols of love painfully underscored the emptiness she felt.

It was snowing when she drove back to the cabin. The flakes were fluffy and dime-sized, and created a magical window through which to view the mountains. It was because of this surreal curtain of snow that Brooke didn't believe her eyes when she saw a huge, white banner with a billboard-sized red heart hanging from the top of the cabin porch. She parked the car, went up to the porch, and placed her fingertips on the heart. The silky cloth moved under her touch. Indeed, it was real.

She placed her key in the cabin door, but it was already open. A fire crackled in the hearth. Around the room everywhere, on the mantel, the tables, even on the floor, were vases of red and white carnations. The air was filled with their perfume. Brooke gasped in surprise and wonder.

She began searching the room for a card, a clue that would reveal the identity of the donor. She looked in each vase, but to no avail.

"The people of Choctaw Hollow shouldn't have done this," she said aloud, throwing out her arms in a gesture of futility.

"They didn't do it. I did," a familiar male voice said.

Brooke whirled to find Drew standing in the doorway of the cabin, his substantial frame almost filling it. His face glowed from the cold.

She walked slowly toward him, unsure he was really there, knowing she'd wanted him so much that she might be imagining him. She stood before him. "You did this? Why?"

The blue in his eyes deepened as he studied her face. "Why does any man give a woman flowers on Valentine's Day?"

She stared at him. Yet something in her heart held her back. She was afraid to believe that the question was merely a rhetorical one.

He took a step toward her and pulled her into his arms. "I did it because I love you, Brooke."

She melted against him, pressing her cheek against his broad chest and feeling the rapid beating of his heart. Then she pulled away and looked into his eyes. They were cloudy with emotion. "Oh, I love you." Her voice was shaky. "But I thought... People, no matter how privileged, can't have everything they want, and I didn't think you wanted me."

He pulled her against him and kissed her forehead, her nose, then finally her mouth. The kiss was filled with a passion and depth that made her heart leap wildly. He pulled away and punctuated the kiss with a brush of his lips against her cheek.

"I've always wanted you, from the moment you regained enough consciousness in my clinic to give me all that spit and sass," he said, brushing his thumb over her bottom lip. Then, when I found out who you were, you were like forbidden fruit. We were of two different worlds and I knew that you wouldn't want any part of mine, at least on a permanent basis. You see, I'd been through something like this before."

Brooke listened as he told briefly how Cheryl had wanted the glitter of the city more than she wanted him.

"So here you came, full of ambition and destined to go on to better things. I didn't dare set myself up for another fall, yet much to my grief, it happened again. I didn't realize how strong my feelings were until they found your raincoat floating downstream."

Holding both his hands in hers, she pressed them against her face.

"To protect my own feelings, I tried to convince myself that you would never make it here, that you were too accustomed to luxury to stick it out. But you kept proving me wrong. You gave up a chance for an exhibit to stay here. You risked your life for Thaney. You did things for this town that no one has done before. I just simply ran out of defenses except to try to distance myself from you. But there's no escaping from what's in a man's heart."

She slipped her arms around his neck. "Drew, there will be other opportunities for exhibits, but right now, all I want is to be here with you," she said. "You and the people of Choctaw Hollow are also the art and the beauty in my life."

His lips moved to her ear. "Does that mean you'll marry me?" he whispered.

"Oh, yes," she said, her heart taking flight.

He lifted her off her feet and twirled her around. "Do you think Grandmama would approve?"

"She'll love you, Drew. I promise. Having a doctor in the family to listen to her latest symptoms will make her ecstatic."

He laughed softly and kissed her once again.

Outside, Thaney stood with his nose pressed against the window. With a hand clamped over his mouth, he suppressed a giggle.